John B. Meredith

Directory for Richland County

with important statistics and historical facts connected with the pioneer

life of early settlers - being an appendix to the author's practical map of

Richland County

John B. Meredith

Directory for Richland County
with important statistics and historical facts connected with the pioneer life of early settlers - being an appendix to the author's practical map of Richland County

ISBN/EAN: 9783337291730

Printed in Europe, USA, Canada, Australia, Japan

Cover: Foto ©Andreas Hilbeck / pixelio.de

More available books at **www.hansebooks.com**

RICHLAND COUNTY
DIRECTORY AND HISTORY,
WITH SKETCHES OF THE
PIONEER LIFE OF EARLY SETTLERS.

PART FIRST.

(To be continued in Magazine Form.)

RAILROAD TIME TABLES FOR DECEMBER, 1870.

This work, with the Magazine numbers which are to fellow and form part of it, will enable us to keep the people posted on the Time Tables for all the Rail Roads passing through Richland county.

Passenger trains leave Mansfield as follows:

P. F. W. & C. RAIL ROAD.
TRAINS GOING WEST.

Lightning.	9:03 A. M.
Mail,	4:22 P. M.
Express,	6:52 P. M.
Express,	10:32 P. M.

TRAINS GOING EAST.

Express.	5:00 A. M.
Mail,	6:40 A. M.
Express,	10:05 A. M.
Lightning.	7:17 P. M

The Mail runs no further west than Crestline. **J. S. MORRIS, Ag't**

A. and G. W. RAILWAY.
TRAINS GOING EASTWARD.

Express,	5:00 A. M.
Accommodation,	7:50 A. M.
Day Express and Mail,	1:43 P. M.
Accommodation,	2:43 P. M.

TRAINS GOING WEST.

Mail,	10:17 A. M.
Accommodation.	1:30 P. M.
Express,	10:32 P. M.

M. B. BUSHNELL, Ag't.

B. and O. RAILROAD.
GOING SOUTH.

Night Freight,	11:30 P. M.
Freight and Passenger,	4:50 P. M.
Mail and Express,	9:52 A. M.
Baltimore Express,	10:18 P. M.

B. & O. R. R. GOING NORTH.

Chicago Express,	7:05 P. M.
Mail and Express,	3:27 P. M.
Freight and Passenger,	12:55 P. M.
Night Freight	3:36 A. M.
Through Freight,	8:40 A. M.

Freight trains have accommodations for passengers.

FRANK JANES, Ag't.

C. C. C. & I. Railroad Time Table.

Passenger trains leave the several stations named below as follows:

TRAINS GOING SOUTH.

Stations.	Cin'l Exp.	N. Y. Exp.	N. O. Exp.
Cleveland,	7:15 A. M	3:00 P. M	7:30 P. M
Shelby,	9:42 A. M	6:15 P. M	9:58 P. M
Crestline,	10:10 A. M	6:30 P. M	10:25 P. M
Galion,	10:30 A. M	6:42 P. M	10:35 P. M

TRAINS GOING NORTH.

Columbus,	11:10 A. M	2:35 A. M	1:00 P. M
Galion,	1:06 P. M	4:35 A. M	6:15 P. M
Crestline,	1:30 P. M	4:55 A. M	6:50 P. M
Shelby,	1:48 P. M	5:42 A. M	7:09 P. M

Besides the above, the Galion Express leaves Galion at 5:25, Crestline 6:30, and Shelby at 6:58.

DIRECTORY

FOR

Richland County,

WITH

IMPORTANT STATISTICS

AND

HISTORICAL FACTS

CONNECTED WITH

THE PIONEER LIFE OF EARLY SETTLERS:

BEING

An Appendix to the author's Practical Map of Richland
County, which embraces the great improvements
secured to him by copy right.

—

BY JOHN B. MEREDITH.

MANSFIELD, OHIO:
1870.

ILLUSTRATIVE DIAGRAM.

4a6	4a5	4a4	4a3	4a2	4a1	4N	4b1	4b2	4b3	4b4
3a6	3a5	3a4	3a3	3a2	3a1	3N	3b1	3b2	3b3	3b4
2a6	2a5	2a4	2a3	2a2	2a1	2N	2b1	2b2	2b3	2b4
1a6	1a5	1a4	1a3	1a2	1a1	1N	1b1	1b2	1b3	1b4
6W	5W	4W	3W	2W	1W	✱	1E	2E	3E	4E
1c6	1c5	1c4	1c3	1c2	1c1	1s	1d1	1d2	1d3	1d4
2c6	2c5	2c4	2c3	2c2	2c1	2s	2d1	2d2	2d3	2d4
3c6	3c5	3c4	3c3	3c2	3c1	3s	3d1	3d2	3d3	3d4

The above Diagram represents part of a county divided into sections one mile square, with a star [✱] to designate the location of the county seat. It will be seen that the *systematic number* placed on each section, gives the miles and course from the county seat to the center of the section. These numbers are fully explained both on the Map and in the Directory, where they are used to designate the location of whatever is numbered.

It is proper to state that this Directory and the author's Practical Map of Richland County, form two parts of the same work, neither of which would be complete without the other. The map was published with the intention of embracing both in *an atlas*, and the Directory is only changed to *book form* to render it more convenient for reference.

THE GREAT MAP IMPROVEMENTS.

By the great improvements secured to the author by copy right, including his *systematic numbers*, he is now able to furnish a combined MAP AND DIRECTORY for about $5, which will not only embrace double the information contained in the large County Maps recently published by other authors and sold for $10 per copy, but the information is obtained in one-fourth of the time. The names of persons and places being alphabetically arranged outside, affords a ready-reference to locations, and entirely obviates the necessity of making maps inconveniently large.

RICHLAND COUNTY DIRECTORY.

In this Directory the *systematic number* of the section in which a farm is located is placed opposite the owner's name, and that number gives the miles and course from the county seat to the section. The letters a, b, c and d, designate courses, and the figures give the distance, as follows:

A. North West.—The miles North are *before* and the miles West *after* a.
B. North East.—The miles North are *before* and the miles East *after* b.
C. South West.—The miles South are *before* and the miles West *after* c.
D. South East.—The miles South are *before* and the miles East *after* d.

Names of Land Owners in Richland County, with the miles and course from Mansfield to the land of each.

Arnold John	(*Bloominggrove* tp.)	10a1	Applegate Joseph	5d8, 5d9
Allen Gustavus		11N	Applegate W C	7d9
Amsbaugh George		14b1	Algire John	(Perry) 12c4
Adams Andrew		12a1	Amas J.G.	11c4
Adams Margaret		15b1	Adbms S H	(Plymouth) 13a9
Anderson Charles	(Butler tp.)	11b3	Amsbaugh Adam	10a10
Adams Isaac	(Cass)	12a5	Atkins Henry	15a9
Arnold Wm.	(Jackson)	9a4	Andrews Adam	10a8, 11a8
Arnold George		9a3	Armstrong Henry	14a8 & 15a8
Arnold John P.		9a4&9a5	Ashbaugh Christ.	15a8
Augustine Daniel		5a4&5a5	Arter Geo.	(Sandusky) 3a9
Aungst Dan'l	(Jefferson)	10c1	Anderson David	(Sharon) 8a8
Aungst Samuel		13d3&9s	Anderson A D & J	8a8, 8a9
Andrews Lyman		9s	Arter Michael	4a8, 4a9
Alexander H.	10c1, 10c2, 10s	Ardner Michael	6a10
Aungst Christian		10c1	Ackerman M A	6a9
Aungst Geo. (heirs)		11d1, 12d2	Au Christ.	(Springfield) 1a7
Armstrong Hezekiah	13c1, 14c1	Au Henry	1a3, 3a5
Armstrong Joshua	13c1, 14c1	Andrew Wm	2c7, 3a8
Armstrong J. W.	14d1, 13s	Ashbaugh Harvey	3a7, 4a7
Armstrong Isaac		14d1	Appleman James	1c4, 1d2
Aungst G W		11d1, 12d2	Aten John	(Troy) 3c5, 4c5
Andrews Geo.	(Madison)	1b3	Amsbaugh N & W H	4c3
Armstrong James		1c2	Andrews L	(Washington) 8s
Aungst Samuel		3a1	Andrews Jacob	8d1
Au S & J		1W	Allen John W	6s
Au Jacob	(Mifflin)	5E	Armstrong S P	6d3
Amsbaugh H.		2d4	Amsbaugh Christ	3c2
Allen Alanson	1d6, 2d4	Anderson James	4c1
Andrews David	(Monroe)	7d8	Allender Thomas	(Weller) 4b2

Ansor O ... (Worthington) 11d7	Bollman Jacob 5b1
Andrews T B 12d4	Burt Ebenezer 4a2
Airhart Henry 12d4	Bell Samuel 4N
Alexander D W 9d8	Bushey David 8a1, 8N
Alexander R & Tucker 9d8, 9d9	Boyce Alexander 7a2
Alexander Robert 9d7, 9d8	Blocker Jonas .... (Jackson) 9a4
Alexander George 9d8	Briner Henry 9a4
Brobst John ... (Bloom'grove) .. 13b1	Briner John 9a4
Burgoyne George 10a2	Bloom Samuel 9a5
Bricker Levi 10a1, 10a2, 10N	Bushey Abraham 5a4
Binchour Simon 12a2	Briner Jacob 9a6
Beattie Eli .... (Butler) 14b5	Bricker Isaac 8a5, 6a4
Bell Wm 15b2	Bricker Levi 8a3
Beverage A 14b5	Bricker Henry 7a4
Beattie Wm 14b4	Bricker Wm 6a5, 7a6
Braner James 14b5	Barton Henry 7a6
Brink Margaret 13b4	Barnes Patrick 8a3
Beverage James 12b5	Beverstock J A 6a5
Brown Hugh 10b5	Boner David ...... (Jefferson) ... 10s
Backenstow Henry 15b3	Beach A J 9s
Bowers Robert 15b3	Bonham Samuel 9s
Black James ... (Cass) 13a3, 14a3	Bixler Samuel 10s
Bevier J D 14a6	Baker Isaac 10d1, 10s
Bealman Christian 14a5	Boner Mary 9c1
Bowman George 14a5	Burkholder Henry ... 13d3
Bomgardner J W 14a4	Burkholder Jacob 12d2
Broach Peter 13a4	Bear Henry 11c2, 12c1
Bevier J E 13a5	Beal Matilda 12c2
Bevier Lewis 13a5	Beal David 12d1
Bevier Rebecca 12a6	Beal Gotlieb 13cs
Buck Roaert 12a4, 12a5	Bollinger Rudolph 12c1, 12c2
Bilestine Michael 11a4	Bean Joseph 12d1
Bushey Jacob 11a6	Beam Frederick 14s
Briggs Wm 12a5, 11a6	Ball Hiram (heirs) 12d3
Bushey Abraham jr 10a6, 9a6	Bevington Sarah . 13d3
Buck John 10a4	Brown Asa ... 13d2
Bricker Levi 10a3	Baker Peter 9d2
Bevier John 10a4, 14a4	Beal Samuel 13s, 13d1
Bodley Henry 11a6	Bristow Perry ..... (Madison) 3a1
Boardman (heirs) 15a3	Burns, Geddis & Smith 1s
Black John 15a4	Bristor T G 2W
Bray Elijah 15a4	Bristor Thomas 2b1
Backenstow Henry 13a4, 14a4	Bell John (heirs) 1b1
Baker Joshua .... (Franklin) 9a1	Bell Peter 1W
Bear Jacob 9a2	Balliet Stephen 2E
Bricker Tobias 8a3	Bushnell Wm 2d2, 5a2
Bricker Levi 8a2, 8N	Blecker Wm ... 3b2
Brown David 6b1	Bell David H 3E
Boyce Andrew 7a1, 7a2	Bush Jacob 3b2
Boyce Rowland 6a1	Boals David ..... (Mifflin) 2b6
Boyce John D 6N	Bruhaker|Daniel 2b5, 3b5
Boyce Isaiah 6b1	Bear Benjamin 2b6
Bradley Wm 7a2	Balliet Jonas 1b7, 2b7
Bradley Jane 4b1	Bolliet Jacob 1b7
Bringham John 4a2	Boals James 1b6
Boggs Rachel 6a2	Boals Isaiah 1b6, 6E
Boggs Wm 5a2	Barr Fred'k ... 1d7

Barr Samuel	1d7	Bechte D	11a9, 12a9
Bell Anthony	1d5	Briggs George	12a9
Balliet H S	1d4	Briggs Robert	14a7
Balliet Joseph	1d4	Blackman P	10a9, 11a10
Balliet Henry	2d5, 2d6	Bodley M M	13a10
Brindle John	3b6	Bilestine Joseph	14a10
Balliet Solomon	2d5	Bloom Jacob S	10a9
Balliet John	2d4	Baughman Daniel	15a7
Baker L S (Monroe)	3d8	Brink George	15a7, 15a8
Brubaker Samuel	3d7	Bender Jos (Sandusky)	3a10
Barger R B	3d5	Baker Jacob	10W
Bare David	3d5	Baker Martha	10W
Baker Henry	4d5	Bortner Henry	10W, 1c10
Balliet David	5d5, 4d6	Bonnett M W	1c9
Basore David	4d7	Buckwalter John	1c10
Bretty David	5d8	Bliley Bbraham	2c9
Bretty Catherine	5d5	Baker Amos	3a9, 3a10
Basore George	5d7	Baker Henry	1a10
Baughman Abraham	7d8	Bosler Michael	2a10
Baughman Aaron	7d7	Beam Michael	2c10
Berry O A	8d4	Boals & Co	1a10
Berry Jacob	7d5, 8d5	Barr Harrison	1c10
Berry Adam	8d6	Bloom S S (Sharon)	9a7
Berry Benjamin	8d6	Boals David	4a7
Berry C & C	7d5	Bargahiser Levi	9a8
Baughman Gideon	7d5	Bargahiser Jacob senr	7a8
Byerly George	8d4, 8d5	Buckingham C	7a8, 7a9
Balliet D & A	3d6	Bailey Harvey	5a7, 5a8
Bahle P & J	5d8, 5d9	Bailey Wm	5a7
Balliet Paul	4d9	Bailey J H	5a8
Black Joel (Perry)	11c4	Bowman Peter	5a7
Bowers Isaac	10c3	Brubaker Jacob A	9a9
Bissell Joseph	13c4	Brubaker Harrison	9a10
Bissell Emanuel	13c4	Brubaker Isaac	9a10
Baker Christian	12c3	Brown Samuel	7a10
Baker Samuel	12c3	Brown Martin	4a10, 5a10
Bull T K	11c3	Brannan Patrick	7a10
Baughman J F	9c4	Briggs Jesse	9a9
Buckingham D	9c5	Bennet Wm	6a9
Bowers Michael	9c2	Boardman Elizabeth	5a9
Bigbee George	14c4, 14c5	Bowers John K	4a9
Broadrick Jonathan	14c4	Boals Charles (Springfield)	2c5
Bissell Geo	13c5	Brant David	3a7, 3a8
Baughman Annie	9c4	Brooks William	3a6
Bevier Sarah (Plymouth)	12a9	Bloom Uriah	3a8
Bevier John	14a7	Berger David	1a3
Bevier Rebecca	12a7, 13a7	Barnhard David	3a7
Bevier Edward	13a10	Bean Michael	2a8
Bevier Caleb	11a9, 12a9, 12a10	Barrow J H	2a5
Bevier Joseph	15a9	Barrow Edward	2a5
Brinkerhoff Josiah	15a8	Booser Henry	1a5, 2a5
Brink Abraham	14a8	Barr Samuel	1a3
Beelman Joseph	13a8	Bell David	3W
Brown James	10a8	Bitner David	2c8
Broadhead H J	13a9, 13a10	Bernard G W & S	1c6
Bodley Jesse	13a10	Brown A R	1c5
Brumback Henry	15a8	Brant D	3a7

Name		Ref	Name		Ref
Barr David	(Troy)	3c4	Conley Samuel		14a1
Barr William		3c4	Cleland Amaziah		15a1
Bowers Rebecca		3c7	Cleland Wm	14N, 15N, 14a1,	15a1
Boals Jos		3c7,3c8	Cleland John		14N
Brown Thomas L		4c3,4c4	Curtis C		14a1
Beverstock A B		3c4,7c3	Crouse William	12N,	13N
Barnett Martha A		5c5	Callen Jefferson		10b1
Brannan John		6c5	Chew Amon		12a1
Bull Ephraim		8c4	Chew George (heirs)		12a2
Bozer John		8c3	Chew John		12a2
Bozer Michael		8c3	Chew Ezekiel	12a2,	13a2
Brannan G L		7c3	Chew Joseph		12a2
Barnett Andrew		5c5	Cummings Jas	10b1,	11b1
Beer Peter		3c6	Cribling Joseph		10a1
Bowers Samuel		7c3,8c4	Cribling Jacob		10N
Bently Robert	(Washington)	3d2	Crawford William	10N,	11N
Bowers George		8c1,8b1,8s	Clawson Talmadge		11N
Baker Hiram		4d2,4d3	Cracraft C (guardian)		11a2
Baker Isaac		7d1	Cline Elizabeth		10b1
Baker David		7d2	Conley Samuel		14a1
Braden Samuel		4d2	Couty George	(Butler)	15b5
Braden Elizabeth		4d2	Chambers John	15b4,	15b5
Beattie Robert		3c1	Copeland John	14b4,	14b3
Beverstock A B		5c2,6c2,7c2	Classon John	12b5,	13b5
Bell Robert Sen		4c2,5c2	Clayburg Jacob	13b3, 13b4,	14b3
Bell Robert Jr		4c2	Clayburg Isaac		10b4
Bell Catherine		3d3	Church James		10b5
Buher Peter J		6d1	Cline S		10b3
Brown Robert	5c1,6c1,7c1		Crabbs Abraham		13b3
Brown Wm L		7c1	Chamberlain Josiah		14b1
Boden Joseph		8c2	Christofel Nancy		12b5
Bowland Geo W		8c2	Coleman D W C		14b5
Bowers Nancy		8c1	Collin William		14b5
Bowers Frederick		8d1	Coble Samuel		10b5
Boals John	(Weller)	4b3	Crabbs J F	10b4,	10b5
Brown Joseph C		7b2	Cline Milton		12b2
Backenstow Jacob		9b2	Cook Alexander		15b3
Boyce Isaiah		9b2	Clay Tracy	(Cass)	13a4
Burns Andrew		6b3	Carmichal F & J		15a5
Brown H W		9b2	Clock Arch		13a3
Beal John	(Worthington)	13d4	Crawford James		13a3
Bevington Sarah		14d4	Crawford John		12a3
Butterbaugh Jos		13d5,14d5	Crawford David	12a3,	12a4
Bemiller Philip		12d7	Crabbs Jacob	12a6,	13a6
Bemiller John		12d5,12d6	Cline Jacob		10a5
Bemiller Val		12d7	Clark Z J		13a5
Bell H		11d6,11d7	Cupenburg A		15a6
Bell R W		11d7	Cox Isaac		11a4
Byerly Susan		9d4	Crall John	(Franklin)	8a1
Bishop Wm		9d7	Crum John	7a2, 8a2,	8a1
Buzzard D B		9d8	Crall Joshua	4N,	4b1
Beal Hannah		14d5	Charles Stephenson		7a1
Beal D S		13d4	Clark Frederick		7a2
Cobban Jas	(Bloom'grove)	14b1	Clark George		8a2
Clinesmith B		15b1	Clay John		7a2
Clinesmith Wm		11a1	Copeland William		6a1
Conley Joseph		15a1	Cope John		4a2

Name	Location
Cline Henry	9b1
Cline B F	4a1
Cline Jacob	4a1
Cook Wm (Jackson)	9a3
Cline Jacob	9a5
Cline Wm	9a6
Cutler Barney	8a5, 9a5
Collier Thomas	8a6
Cooper Jacob	8a4
Clark David F	7a5
Clark Calvin	6a5, 7a5, 7a6
Clark Samuel A	6a6
Cooper Daniel	5a4, 6a4, 6a5
Creigh D W	5a6
Craighead Daniel	4a3
Conley James	4a3
Cairns Robert	4a3
Cooper William	6a4
Cook William D	9a3
Collier Amos (Jefferson)	13d3
Charles Christian	10s
Charles Hiram	10s, 10d1
Cleland James	13s
Colley Allen	9d1, 10d1
Campbell John	9c1
Cornern William	10c2
Cross Geo W.	12s, 12c1
Cotsmoyer John	13a3
Conolly John	14s
Cassel Henry R	13d3
Charles W F	11d1
Cutler Robert	14c1
Cate Henry	9d3
Charles Jane (Madison)	3b2
Cole R	3b2
Cole Reuben	1b2
Croft Thomas	1b1
Cassell George	3N
Crooks B (heirs)	3a2
Crooks James	2a2
Cunningham D	2a2
Christian E	1b1
Condon Elisha	2W
Creigh Sarah M	1a2
Crouch B M	2W
Case Joseph	3N
Chandler Jacob	1a1
Coulter James	1c2
Coulter Robert	1d2
Cotner Jacob	3a1
Crider Tobias	1b3
Cookston Jesse	1d3
Campbell James	1d2
Calhoun John.	1d2
Clark James	1c1
Culbertson J H	2s
Cortright C M	2c1
Cromer Elizabeth	2d1
Cline John	1s
Cline John jr	2N
Cline Joseph	2a2
Conaway Charles (Mifflin)	2d6
Charles Amanda	3b7
Crider Tobias	2b4
Crider Jacob	2b7
Cautman C	1b5
Chew James	2d4
Coulter William	1d4
Cline Lewis	3b6
Culler J L (Monroe)	4d7
Cutler Andrew	3d7, 4d6
Culler Michael	3d9, 4d7
Culler Catherine	4d6, 5d7
Culler John (heirs)	4d7
Culler George	4d7, 5d7
Culler & Kiefer	4d8
Chew James	3d4
Crone Jacob	4d4, 5d4, 5d5
Crawford David	7d8
Chew Washington	5d7, 6d6, 6d7
Chew Samuel	5d7
Crone John	6d6
Coulter Miltzer	6d4
Craig John	7d5
Charles John S	7d4
Charles Robert	8d4
Culler A	8d5
Calhoun Thomas	8d9
Cole John	8d4
Charles George P	7d4
Cline B F (Perry)	11c4
Cline Betsey	11c3
Coover Daniel (heirs)	10c5
Clark Lydia	11c3
Carson Wm	11c3
Coon Susan (heirs)	10c3
Coon Jacob	10c3
Culp Jacob & D	13c3, 14c3
Cary John (heirs)	13c3
Coon George	13c4
Chamberlain E	14c4
Courson Wm	11c5
Culp Samuel	13c3
Cutler James (Plymouth)	14a7
Case A	15a7, 15a8
Conklin Wm	14a8
Conklin James	13a7
Conklin Charles	15a8
Cline William	11a7
Champion C	10a9, 11a8, 11a9
Champion John	11a10
Champion W C	10a9
Cain William	14a10
Clark John	14a9

Name	Code	Name	Code
Constance B E	12d5	Douglass John J	7d6
Cleaver John	12d4, 13d4	Dounnan Wm	7d4, 8d4
Craig James A.	12d5	Darling Wm	8d8
Clapper Samuel	10d6, 11d6	Darling G H	8d9
Dunlap John …(Bloom'grove)	14X	Darling Abraham	8d9
Dickerson Thomas	13a2, 14a2	Darling John	8d9
Dennison Rebecca	13b1, 14b1	Dome Samuel	7d9
Devoe Loxley	11a1	Dome Louisa	7d9
Davidson John	13b1	Dome Henry	8d6
Davidson Peter …(Butler)	13b2	Drake Thomas …(Perry)	12c4
Dobbin John	14b3, 15b3	Drew Joseph	13c3
Dancer J B 11b3, 12b4, 12b5, 13b6		Dyer Bracket	13c3
Davis John	11b4, 12b4	Dyer Samuel B	13c3
Deihl Samuel ..(Cass)	14a3	Dayley Harvey	13c3
Dick Levi	11a5, 12a5	Dyer O P	13c3
Dick Josiah	12a5	DuBois A C (Plymouth)	15a7, 15a8
Dick George jr	11a3	Downend Joseph	11a7, 11a8
Dick George	10a4, 10a5	Dalton John	12a7
DuBois H G	15a6	Duncan Elizabeth	11a7
Delancey Peter	13a3	Devoe Levi	14a10
Dickerson John	13a6	Devoe Elijah	14a10, 15a10
Downend Joseph	12a5	Droneberger E	15a10
Downend Thomas	13a6	Doty James	13a9
Darling Wm	11a4	Dewitt C O	13a10
Devinney M M F	15a6	Dawson John	11a10, 13a7
Dalton & Fitzsimmons	11a6	Dick John T	15a8
Delancey Jacob	13a4	Devinney John	15a8
Dunlap Thomas …(Jackson)	9a3	Day Harvey ..(Sandusky)	2c10
Dick Harmon	9a6	Day Ezra	2c10
Davis John	8a6	Dickerson John	3a9
Drake John	7a5, 7a6	Dickerson Asa	3a9
Drake William	7a5	Delp Philip	1c10
Dougal John C	4a6	Doty Joseph (Sharon)	4a7
Dick George	9a6	Duncan Abraham	5a8
Darby John	4a6	Douglass Wm	8a10
Donnell Samuel (Jefferson)	9d1	Douglass John	7a10
Dean John F	10c1, 9s, 10s	Dollinger Henry	5a9
Donought Amos	14d2	Dick Harmon	9a7
Donought William	13d1	Doty John	9a7
Divilbiss David	13b2	Dempsey John	4a8, 8a7, 9a8
Detwiler John	9d2	Dougal John …(Springfield)	2a5
Dehaven Joseph	14s	Dougal John C	2a6, 3a6, 2a8
Dickey Samuel	12s	Dougal Charles	2a6
Durben Nancy	13d3	Dougal Samuel	2a5
Dunshee Thomas	9e1	Davidson James	2a4
Drew A E	14c2	Daniels M	5W
Drew Anson	13e2	Dillie Stephen I.	2c7
Day Matthias …(Madison)	1E	Day Moreas	2c5
Dunkle John	1a2	Dixon James	1c6, 6W
Dickerson Thomas	2s	Dickson Henry (Troy)	3c3, 4c3
DeHart Wm	2d2	Day Harvey C	3c5
Dillon Samuel	2d2	Dillie Aaron	3c7
Dice Daniel	2d1	Dillie John	8c4
Dickson & Byrd	1c1	Douglass Samuel	6c5, 7c5
Dennis John	2d2, 2d3	Danshee Thomas	7c5, 7c4
Donnan Margaret	5N	Dill Wm (Washington)	7d1
Dent Leonard (Monroe)	5d5	Day Amos	3s

Name	Ref	Name	Ref
Derman George	5c1	Ford William	12b3
Dean D W	6d2	Ford George (Cass)	12a4
Daub Henry	8d3	Flemming John	15a6
Dearduff John	5c2	Fletter J M	11a4
Dixon Henry	3c2	Frieze Daniel	11a4, 11a5
Dennis William H	3d3	Firoved Levi	11a5
Dennis John	4d3	Fickes Wesley	10a5
Dix Jacob	3c2, 4c2	Foglesonger Jeremiah	12a6
Dellenbaugh C (Weller)	5b3	Frazer Esther	14a4
Dobbs William	6b2, 6b3, 6b4	Ferree William (Franklin)	7b1
Dixon J J	7b4	Fackler Joseph	9N
Dixon Sarah	7b4	Fiddler John	7a2
Darling J (Worthington)	9d9	Furgnson W A	8N
Davis Abner	10d8, 10d9, 12d9	Fackler Mary & Martin	7a1
Darling Robert	9d9	Fisher John	4a1
Darling William	9d8	Foulks William	9b1
Dougherty Charles	9d4	Finicle Solomon	4a2
Dickey Daniel	13d4	Furgnson Isaac (Jackson)	6a5
Davy George	10d7	Finicle David	4a5, 8a6
Divilbiss David	11d4, 12d4	Finicle John	6a3, 6a4
Divilbiss Simon	12d9, 14d4	Finicle George	6a3
Dutton Warren	14d4	Foster R P	7a6
Deck Abram	14d9	Feighner Solomon	6a6
Duncan John	13d6	Fike Isaac (Jefferson)	12c2
Evans G (All Townships)	5a1	Fitting F B	9d1, 9s, 10s
Earnest John	3N	Fisher Daniel	10d1
Egerly Abraham	4c2	Flaharty Nicholas	10s, 10d1
Englehart George	5s	Fitting Geo H	13c1
Etz Philip	8d3	Flemming George	9d2
Eby Jacob	1b5, 7E	Fox Daniel	11d2
Eby Samuel	1b4	Fitting A M	12c1
Eby Isaac	7E	Fry Christopher	13d1
Ernsberger Elias	2d7	Farquhar A G	14c2
Evans Washington	1c8	Files Nathaniel	14c1
Evans D E	3a5	Fisher Jacob	14s
Enlow Aaron N	7c4	Fitting Geo H	12c1
Eckert P & J	5c5, 7c5, 8c5	Fry Thomas	13d1
Eckert Daniel	7c5, 7c6, 8c5	Frederick Eli	10d3
Eckert David	7c5, 8c5	Frederick C P	10d3
Eckert Samuel	8c5	Finney Thomas (Madison)	1c2
Erwin Ezekiel	4d6, 5d6	Finney W S	2c1
Flook Casper (Blooom'grove)	4a1	Finney William	2c2
Finck Stephen	13N	Finney Elijah	2s
Fry James	12a2	Frost William	2d1
Foulks Geo A	12N	Finicle Solomon	3a2
Foulks Henry W	11N	Fox Daniel	2b3
Furguson Harrrison	10b1	Flemming Wm (Mifflin)	2b5, 3b5
Fox Tobias	11N	Flemming J G	2b5, 3b5
Foulks M A (Butler)	12b4	Faltry Moses (Monroe)	3d4
Foulks Hiram	13b4, 13b5	Fox J R	4d8
Forbes Wm	13b4, 14b4	Furguson John	3d7
Ford Elias	12b4	Ferry H B	3d5
Ford Joshua	11b5, 12b5	France E H	3d5
Freeman Daniel	12b5	Faber Peter (Perry)	10c5
Francis John	10b4	Frary Justus	10c5
Ferris John	10b5	Fissell Jacob	12c3, 13c3
Fackler Henry	12b3	Follin Daniel	13c4, 13c5

Name	Location	Name	Location
Gatton Isaac ...	9c1,11c1	Gass John (heirs)	4c4
Gatton Thomas	11d3, 12d3	Goldsmith Jacob	3c8
Gatton Maria	11d2	Gates Robert jr	3c5
Goss J & G	11c2	Goldsmith Asahel	3c8
Gibson Nancy	13c1	Geese Jacob	4c4
Gibson Hiram	14c2	Grubb Thomas J	8c6
Gibson M	14c1	Green Joshua	8c3
Geddis Davis	13c2, 14c2	Glenn John (Washington)	5s
Golloway W	14c2	Gillelan Thomas	5c1
Gribling Anna M (Madison)	3N	Garver Samuel	6s
Garrison William	2b3, 3b3	Grice Thomas	6d1
Gates Jacob	2b1	Gribb David	8c2
Gates Martin.	2b3	Gatton Joseph	7d2
Gates M L	1b3	Gerhart David	8d1, 8s
Gates William	1b3	Gerhart Andrew	8s
Gates Peter	1b3	Gerhart T S	7c2 8c2
Gibbs James ...	1b2	Glenn Samuel (Weller)	8b3
Goldsmith Usher	2c1	Guthrie William	5b3, 5b4
Gates Wm (Mifflin)	3d5	Grimes Adam	7b3, 8b3
Gates J P	1d5	Glenn Hugh (heirs)	8b3
Griffeth Wm	1d6	Gleason A (Worthington)	10d6
Gledhill Walter (Monroe)	3d6	Granwood William	10d6
Gladden Solomon	6d8	Groon Simon	11d9
Gladden Mad	6d8	Garber Samuel	11d8, 12d8, 14d4
Gladden R H	6d8	Gatton Lucy	10d4
Gregg Thomas C	6d8	Greer M	14d6
Griffin Elliott	7d8, 7d9	Garnett George	13d5
Goodhart Jacob (Perry)	10c5	Gender John W	14d5
Gibson Addison	12c3	Greer A	12d4, 12d5
Goss George	10c3	Gunter William	14d5
Garoy John	13c3	Greer James	10d8
Graham J S	14c5	Garber Daniel	13d4
Graham Hiram (Plymouth)	15a8	Garber D	13d5
Griffeth E J	12a10	Garnett Eli	10d8
Griffeth John	12a10	Gueiselmam F	12d8
Griffeth Levi	12a10	Garnett William	9d8
Gipson Stutley	15a9	Hackett H P (Bloom'grove)	13N
Gipson Michael	15a9	Hackett George	12N,13a1,15a1
Genong George	15a9	Hackett William	12a1,12a2
Genong Joel	15a9	Hueston Alexander	15N
Garrison Card	13a10,14a10	Hueston Jane	11b1
Gribben Isaac	14a9	Hueston James	12N
Gorton Joel	13a9	Hunter Andrew	12N
Grandon Susan	13a10, 14a10	Hunter Joseph	12b1
Green Walter	11a10	Hunter Benjamin	12b1
Gates R J (Sandusky)	2a10	Hunbert William	13b1
Gebsonleiter Peter	1c10	Hammon Peter	13a1
Gamble Hugh (Sharon)	6a8	Holtz John	14a2
Garnhart Daniel	9a8, 9a9	Hammon Wm (Butler)	15b5
Garnhart Jacob	9a9, 9a10	Hammon Wilson	15b5
Gunter (heirs)	6a10	Hammon Philip	15b3
Gibson John (Springfield)	1c5	Houston Robert	10b4
Geddis G W	1a5	Houston John	10b4
Gass James R (Troy)	4c3	Hubby Adam	15b2
Gass William	4c3	Hubby Henry	13b2
Gass Benjamin	3c3, 3c4	Hunter Joseph	12b3
Graham D	5c4	Haddox Levi	15b2, 15b3

Henry M A (Cass)	14a4	Harris W. S.	2d2
Hodges H T	14a5, 15a5	Hall Harvey	2a1
Hershiser L	10a5, 10a6	Hess Henry	2a1, 3a1
Hershiser John	10a6	Hoffer J B	3b2
Henry Cyrus	13a3	Hummell Jacob M	2b1
Hodges J Y	15a3	Hade Emanuel	1a1
Heth Samuel	15a3	Hildreth Joseph	2c2
Hughes James (Franklin)	7b1	Hale John Senr (Mifflin)	3b5
Harnley John	7b1, 8b1	Hale Hugh	2b4, 3b4
Hall Robert	5a2	Hagerman Wm	3b4
Haines Benjamin	5a2	Hilton John	3b4
Hecht Peter	4a1	Hout Joseph	2b4, 2b6
Hultz Simon	9a1	Hout George	2b4
Hultz Jacob (Jackson)	8a4	Hout Peter	1b6
Hayes Almon	7a5	Hout John	1b5
Hines Philip	7a6	Hoover Daniel	2b6
Hawk Wm	6a6	Hoover C	2b6
Hornberger Benj'n	5a5, 6a5	Hoover Henry	1b5
Hoffman Daniel	6a4	Hout Daniel	1b5
Hoffman James W	5a4	Hout Wm	2d6
Hartman John F	5a5	Hostetter Joseph	7E
Hartman George	5a5	Henry Samuel (Monroe)	6d6
Hines Frederick	8a4	Henry N S	4d8, 4d9
Henry Daniel	8a4	Hossinger Henry	3d9, 4d9
Holtz George	8a4	Hossinger Jacob & A	3d9
Hagenbach N	8a3	Hastings Joseph	6d5
Hull John	4a5	Hursh Joel	4d6, 5d6
Hayes L C	7a5	Hughes Aaron	7d9
Hill Lewis	5a6	Huston John (heirs)	7d5
Holtz Frederick	9a5	Harter Wm	8d5
Hines B F (Jefferson)	10d1	Hogan Michael	8d8
Harrington A L	9d3	Herring Cyrus	8d6
Harrington Harmon	9s	Horner Barnhart	5d9, 6d9
Howard Otis	9a1, 10s	Herring Phebe	8d6
Hyatt M	11s	Hueston David	6d5
Hamilton Samuel	9s, 14s	Hursh David	5d6
Hosack Adam	13c1	Herzog John	8d8
Hoover Simon	9d3	Hardman James (Perry)	2c4
Hoover Elizabeth	9d3	Hiskey V & M	9c5
Hueston Mary E	13c1	Hiskey Enoch	10c4
Hueston T & J	10c1, 10c2	Hall & Allen	10c5
Hamilton John	11s, 11c1	Halcher John	11c5
Hardesty N	13s	Hardman Anthony	12c5, 13c5
Herron Samuel	12c1	Hines William	13c3, 13c4
Howard Johnston	12s	Hannawalt John	10c3, 10c4
Hartman David	12d2	Hosack Adam	14c5
Henderson A	11c2	Hosack A	14c4
Henderson Wm	13c1	Huntsman Jonathan	12c5
Hiskey E	12c2	Huntsman James	12c5
Hickox W S (Madison)	1E	Hardman George	12c5
Hedges F (heirs)	1d1, 1E	Hardman J jr	12c4
Hursh John	2b3	Hosack John	14c5
Hursh Henry	1b2	Heist Samuel A	12c3
Hedges H. C.	1c1	Huntsman Josiah	13c5
Hunt William	1d3	Hills John J (Plymouth)	15a9
Hamilton Sarah	2d2	Hollenbaugh John	10a7, 10a8
Hall John	2d2	Hutcheson Charles	13a7, 12a8, 12a9

Name	Code	Name	Code
Hardy Charles	12a7, 12a8	Huston Wm. heirs	8b5
Hills Thomas	14a9	Huston John	9b4, 9b5
Hardy John	13a10	Huston Richard	8b5
Hornbeck Derrick	15a7	Hughes Thomas	5b4, 6b4
Hoover John (Sandusky)	1c10	Hughes Robert	6b3
Hatlick P.	9W	Hughes David	6b3
Hardy M R	2c9	Hughes James	7b2, 8b2
Harding W P	3a10	Haverfield Joseph	7b2
Hunter David	3a9	Haislet C (Worthington)	10d6
Hill Lewis	4a10	Henderson J P	9d7
Horning Justice	3a9	Herring F	9d7, 10d7
Hawn Eliza (Sharon)	7a8	Harter Wm.	9d6
Holgate Reuben	7a7, 7a8	Haislet Wm	10d5
Hollenbaugh Benj	9a8	Hammond Thomas	11d6
Hawk Wm.	5a7, 6a7, 7a7	Herring Wm.	10d7
Horning James	4a10	Haislet Samuel	10d8, 12d7
Hines Nicholas	7a10	Hughes John	12d7
Hawkinsmith & Smith	7a10	Hernley John	12d8
Hershiser Samuel	9a7	Haislet James	12d9
Hill John (Springfield)	2a5	Horsefelt S E	13d9
Harris H L	2a5	Hueston Wm	12d5
Hulter John	2a3	Herring Maria	13d6, 13d7
Hout John	1a8	Harris Wm	13d9
Hout Peter	1a8	Hoover Henry	14d7
Hackedorn D A	6W, 7W	Hoover John	13d7 14d7
Hatlick Jacob	1c6	Harvely George	13d6, 13d7
Hildicker Samuel	1a4	Halferty Jacob	14d7, 14d8
Hutchinson S M	1c8	Halferty S heirs	14d7, 14d8
Hartupee Wm	2c5	Halferty J M	14d7
Hardenfield George	4W, 1c4	Hill Daniel	14d9
Hiskey David (Troy)	6c5	Hildebrand Charles	14d9
Hiskey George	7c5, 8c4	Hissong J H	14d4
Hiskey Andrew	6c5	Hittinger J W	13d7
Hiskey Martin	7c5	Hayes John	13d8
Hiskey Mrs. E	8c4	Harter Matthias	14d8
Hunter Wm. (heirs)	3c8	Hammond R J	13d5, 13d6
Hetrick Jacob	8c6	Irwin James (All townships)	6d9
Hosack John	7c3	Irwin Meltzer	6d9
Hunter J W	3c8	Ireland David	4c2
Horn Peter	8c4	Irwin Matthew	13a10
Hull John (Washington)	3d2	Jesson Robert	1b3
Hammet Wm B	4d1, 4d2	Johns B. (heirs)	1N, 2N, 1d1
Hammet John	3d2	Johnson Wm	2d3
Hamilton Harrison	5c1, 6c2	Johns David	1d3
Hunter A S	5d3	Jones J A	2N, 3d1
Hunter George	5c2	Jaques David	1a7, 2a7, 3a7
Hunter Isaac	7d3	Jones Wm	1a3
Heist Benj	4s	Jolly Charles	1c6
Harnley Moses	5c2	Jump Robert	6b2
Harrington L F & Bro	8d1	Jump A O	6b4
Horn Christian (Weller)	4b5	Johnston Michael	8c6
Hagerman James	4b2	Johnston James	4d4
Hagerman Wm	4b4, 4b5	Johnston Robert	5d4
Hetler Henry	4b2	Jarvis Sarah	6a10
Haverfield-Allen	6b3	Johnson Demas	14a1
Huston Robert	7b5	Johns Benjamin	1a10, 3a10
Huston J L	8b5	Johnson George	1a9

Name	Code	Name	Code
Jacoby John	1a9	Kirkpatrick D (heirs)	14a7
Johnston John	11a9, 11a10	Knisely Joseph (Sandusky)	3a10
Johnston Edward	11a9	Koons Daniel	2a9, 2a10
Jones Wm	13a7	Koon Charles	1c9, 9W
Jones Andrew	13a7, 14a7	Kirtner Andrew	2c9
Johnson Wm A	15a7	Kerr Isaiah	9W
Jacobs John	13b1	Kahl Henry (Sharon)	6a8
Kensell J W (Bloom'grove)	13N	Kochenderfer Sarah	6a7, 7a7
Kensell Thomas	13a2	Kahl Susan	7a8
Kunkleman Jacob	10a2	Kerr Jesse	5a7
Kauffman H. (Butler)	10b3	Kerr Robert	7a7, 7a8
Kirk Patrick	11b5, 12b3	Knox Catharine	7a9, 8a9
Kirk E T.	11b3, 11b1	Kerr George S	5a10, 6a10
Koerber J jr (Cass)	14a4	Keller Gregory	5a9, 5a10
Kinsell Sarah.	13a3	Keller Joseph	5a10
Kuhn John.	12a5	Kurtzeman Martin	5a9
Kline Morris (Franklin)	9a2	Kerr Wm	4a9
Kendall John	5a1, 6a1	Kline George	9a9
Kline Henry	8b1, 9b1	Kilgore Joseph Springfield,	2c8
Kline H	1a2	Kunkle George	1a8
Kokenderfer Joseph	9N	Kanaga Elizabeth	5W
Kohler David	9b1	Klinkle George	3a6
Kohler Jacob	4N	Kiles Wm (Troy)	8c4
Kohler Hezekiah	1b1, 5b1	Kirkland Mary J	3c7
Keith Michael	5a1, 6a1	Kirkland James Sr	3c7
Kessell Jacob	8a1	Kraybill Charles	1c3
Keiser Jacob	5a1	Kilgore James	3c3
Keller Joel	4b1	Koch Frederick	3c3
Kuhn Jacob (Jackson)	4a5	Klower J W Washington	5d2
Kerr Mary	8a3, 9a3	Kohiser Lewis	7c4
Kerr Wm	8a3, 9a6	Kohiser John P	8d1, 8d2
Kirkpatrick Jeremiah	5a3	Kenedy David	3c4
Kanaga W W (Jefferson)	11d3	Kenedy John C	1c4
Kanaga John	12d2, 13d2	Kohiser Peter W	1s
Kanaga Wm	10d3	Krabill Jacob	5c4
Kohiser H P	9d3	Knox John	7c4, 7c2
Keith John T. (Madison)	3N	Knox J & W B	8c4
Keiser Michael	1a2	Kell Elijah	8c4
Koogle Jacob Mifflin	6E	Kohiser Mary	6d4
Kahler Daniel	2b5, 3b5	Keistetter Anthony	6d4
Keefer Jacob	1d6	Kirtz Jesse	1c4
Kahler Frederick	3b7	Knepley Jacob	3d4, 4d4
King Daniel	1d5, 1d6	Kirkwood Charles Weller	8b2
King & Co	1d4	Kirkwood Isaac	8b3
Kurtz John	2d7	Kramer Abraham	8b5
Kenton Polly (Monroe)	7d4	Kale John (Worthington)	13d7
King Christena	3d8	Kanaga Josiah	10d4, 11d4
King Ephraim	3d7	Keller Peter.	10d7
Kaylor Frederick	1d8	Kenton John	13d8
Kerr Hamilton	6d9	Kile A C	12d8
Kinsell Dan'l (Plymouth)	13a8	Kunkle William	12d7
Kirkpatrick Wm	14a7, 15a7	Laser Daniel (Bloom'grove)	10a8
Kuhn John	11a8, 12a8	Laughlin Catherine	11a1
Kuhn Samuel	12a8	Latimore Nancy	11a1
Kuhn J & C	13a7, 13a8	Latimore William	15N
Kendall John	11a8	Lindsey Wilson	11b1
King G W	11a10	Long William R	11b1

Name	Code	Name	Code
Lanson James (Butler)	13b5	Lafferty Uriah	10d3
Latimore George	13b4, 13b5	Lee Ebenezer	4c1
Lyon Wm	15b2	Lenhart Wm	10d2
Latimore James	12b5	Long John (Madison)	1N, 2N
Long David (Cass)	14a3	Lantz Francis	1b3, 2b3
Lantz Margaret	12a3	Lantz Abraham	2b3
Lantz Jacob	12a3	Lewis John F	3N
Lybarger Daniel	10a4	Ludwig Peter	1W
Lybarger Lewis	10a3	Latimore George	2b2
Laser M	10a4	Leightner & Schmutzler	1d2
Laser John	11a3	Leech John	1d1
Laser G W	11a3	Lamberton James	1s
Louternilch C	10a3	Larimer Robert	1c2, 2c2
Longnecker G W	10a6	Larimer James	2c2
Lippey David (Franklin)	5a1	Line David	2b2
Lippey Sarah	5a2	Landis Samuel (Mifflin)	2b5
Lippey John	6a2	Lewis Solomon	4E, 1b6, 1b7
Lehman Samuel L	4a1	Lewis Samuel	1b7
Lehman Christian	4N	Lutz John A	6E
Light John	9a1	Leiter D	1d7, 2d7
Light David	8a1, 8a2	Leiter Jacob (Monroe)	3d6
Light Nicholas	9a1	Leiter David	2d1, 4d1, 5d6
Lantz George	6a2	Leiter Lewis	5d6
Linn Adam	5N	Lafferty Samuel	6d6
Lybarger Uriah A	9a1	Lantz Samuel (Perry)	10c4
Louternilch C	9a2	Lemon Rober heirs	14c3
Leppo Wm (Jackson)	4a4	Lavering Noah	14c5
Laser Jacob	8a4, 9a5, 9a6	Lavering John C	14c5
Laser Samuel	7a4, 8a4	Lipset Robert (Plymouth)	13a7
Laser Catherine	7a3	Lewis Jonathan	12a10
Laser Christian	9a3	Lipset Anthony heirs	13a7
Leppo John	4a4, 5a4	Loveland G W	15a8
Lantz Amos	5a3, 5a1	Loveland D	15a8
Livensperger Daniel	4a6	Lyon Melissa	15a9
Livensperger D	4a3, 4a5	Lovett John (Sandusky)	2a10
Landis John M	8a6, 9a5	Logan D	3c9
Larimore John	4a6, 5a6	Lenhart Jacob	1c9
Lash Philip Jefferson	10c4	Leppo James (Springfield)	3a4
Lefever E J	10d1	Leppo Samuel	2a3
Lockhart Aaron jr	10s	Leppo Wm	2a3, 3a3
Lee James C	9s	Leppo John	2a3, 2a4
Lefever Samuel	10d1	Laird Hester M	5W, 2a5
Lockhart Aaron	10d2, 10d3, 12d1 &c	Livensberger Elizabeth	6W
Lefever W J	13di	Lindsley Israel M	2c4
Linhart Peter	9d2	Logan Wm	2c3, 2c4
Lobach John	10c1	Larimer Josiah	2c3
Lafferty Samuel	11c1, 12c1	Larimer Alexander	1c7
Long Samuel	12c1, 12c2	Lewis Wm (Troy)	4c5
Long Abraham	14d3	Logan Thomas	3c4, 4c4
Leedy Jacob B	13d2	Logan James	3c5
Leedy Daniel	13d2	Leyman Jacob	7c6, 8c5
Leedy Elizabeth	13d1	Lindsley Elizabeth	3c6
Leedy Samuel	14d1	Logan Wm (Washington)	3s
Leedy Lewis K	14d2	Leppo David (heirs)	1d2
Ladd Jacob	11S, 12d2	Lutz Thomas	4d1
Leedy A	14d1, 14d2	Lawrence Charles	6c1
Lafferty John	11d3	Lindsey James	7s

Name	Ref	Name	Ref
Lindsey Rebecca	7W	Markum Joseph	14a5
Labach A W	8d1	Messenger M	12a3, 12a4
Leonhoast Philip	5s	Moore William	12a6, 13a6
Loudenberger Lewis	5s	Moore J L	11a6, 12a6
Linn & Dobbs (Weller)	7b4	McConnell G W	11a5
Leedy A H (Worthington)	13d4	May Henry	11a6
Leeper Ebenezer	10d4	Manger John	10a6
Lockhart Reason	13d7, 14d7	McLauglin W	14a3
Lafferty Uriah	10d4, 11d4	Myers Jacob (Franklin)	5b1
Long Abraham	14d4	Myers Samuel	5N, 5b1
Lamley Gotleib	14d5, 14d6	Martin Alanson	5b1
Lamley Caleb	14d6	Martin Samuel	4a1
Laser Rachel	13d9	Morehead Forgus	7b1
Lisle John	11d7, 11d8	Morthland Abraham	6a2
Lisle A B	10d7, 10d8	Moore John W	7a1
Magaw J C (Bloom'grove)	14N	Miller Michael	4a2
Magaw Martin	14N, 15a1	Miller Peter	4a1
McCombs William	15b1	Monn Joseph C	9a1, 9a2
Middleswarth Daniel	15a2	Matteau Jacob	4b1
Miller William	15a2	March C F	4N
Miller Daniel	45a2	McMeeken James	6N
Miller Michael	10b1, 11b1	Marvin Judith (Jackson)	9a7
Maring Peter	14a2, 15a2	Marvin Stephen	8a6
Miller Samuel	15a2	Miller Isaac H	8a5, 8a6
Meek Robert	14a1	Miller Jonathan	7a3
Meek John	14a2	McDougal Alexander	5a4
Madden Alexander	15b1	Morthland Abraham	5a3, 6a3
Moser H S	15a2	Myers John	5a5
Mohn Leonard	11a2	Matson Uriah	4a5
Morgan Sarah	10N	Morthland John	5a3
Morgan Simon	10N	Mowry Philip (Jefferson)	9d2
Morgan Mary	10N	Morrow John 12s, 9d1, 12d1	
McLaughlin John	15a2	McKinney M J	13c1
Moore John (Butler)	15b5	Morris James	12c2
Madden Alexander 11b2, 11b3, 13b3		Myers Jacob	13d2
McKibben H 12b4, 13b4, 15b4	15b5	McClure Thomas (he rs)	10d1
McKibben Joseph	15b5	McGarvey John	12c1
Murray Edward 12b4, 13b5		Marven Jesse	14c2
McDonald Henry 15b2, 15b3		Mock John	14d2
Middleswarth Samuel	14b2	Mowry James	14c1
Mitchell James	14b2	Moody Miller (heirs)?	9s, 10d1
Morris Benjamin	10b2, 11b2	Measel Peter	9s, 9d1
McMillin Alexander	10b5	Moody Eliza	9d1
Mitchell George	11b2	McKee Johnson (Madison)	1c2
McConley David	12b2	McCullough John	2d1
McBride Alex. (Cass)	15a4	McKee Samuel	1c1
McBride Thomas	15a5	Miller A G (heirs)	1c1
Miller William	14a5	McConnell Matthew	2c2
Matthewson W H 14a4, 14a5		Morehead Robert	2c1
Mozier John 15a4, 15a4		McKinley George	2d2
Meriott Robert 12a4, 13a4		Mentzer George A	1d3
Miller Jacob	15a5	Murphy John F	3a1
Miller Samuel	10a6	McElroy Alexander 3E, 3a2	
Millick Daniel	14a5, 14a6	Maloney Robert	2b2
Millick J A	13a5	McFall Hugh (heirs)	1b1
Mount James 13a6, 14a6		McElroy William	2b1
Mount Andrew	13a6	Morehead R M & P B	2c1

Maglott Adam	(Mifflin)	2d6	Morthlan John	2c9, 2c10, 3c10
Matthews Daniel		3b6	McFarland Joseph	3c9
McConnell William		3b4	Mills A C	2a10
Morehead Calvin	4E, 1b4		McCarty Jeremiah	2a10
Markly David		1b7	May Jonathan ....(Sharon)	8d7
McDermot Mark		1d5	Metsear Pence	5a8, 5a9
Mentzer John		1d4	Metsear Simon	5a10
Miller John & George		1b4	Metsear Anthony	5a10
McSherry John		1d6	Morehead Jedediah	9a9
McBride W		5E	Mohler Jacob	5a8
McBride William ...(Monroe)	5d5		Morse G W	6d7
McBride Ann	5d7, 6d7, 6d8		Most George	5a8, 5a9
McBride Alexander	4d4, 5d4		Myers John	8a10, 9a10
McBride B F	4d4, 5d4		Myers David	8a9, 8a10
Moser Lewis	3d4, 4d4		McMahan Ross	6a10
Miller William N	7d9, 8d9		McMahan Patrick	5a9, 6a10, 7a10
McDermot Wesley		6d7	Miller Marcus	6a10
Manner Jacob	8d7, 8d8		Mott Mary Ann	6a9
Mitchell M C	6d4, 7d4		Mott Peter	6a9
Mowery Isaac		3d8	Miller Jacob	5a9
McKee Robert		3d6	Mitchell Joseph	4a10
McFarland George		3d4	Mouse Henry (heirs)	4a10
Mentzer Isabel		3d4	Mickey Thomas	8a10, 9a10
Marks Abraham		4d6	Moulton N S	8a9
Marlow Jane		5d7	Metcalf J J	8a9
McFarland Andrew		5d4	Mack John	8a8
McNeal M		6d5	Most Joseph	5a9
McDaniel R		7d8	Marvin Stephen	8a7
Mowery A & M		7d4	Myers Samuel ...(Springfield)	3a3
Miller Milo		7d9	Muthersbaugh Jacob	3a4
Miller Christian ...(Perry)	10c4		Matson John	3a5
McFarren Henry	11c5, 13c3		McKnight John B	3a7, 3a8
McCrory Elizabeth		14c4	McKnight Margaret	1c8
Markward Samuel		11c5	Musselman Jacob	2a8, 3a8
McDonald Daniel		11c5	McCoughey Joseph	2a4
Marsh Benjamin		13c4	Marshall Samuel	1a4
McKinley Alexander		9c3	Marshall James	1a5, 5W, 6W
McDonald Joseph		14c3	Mitchell George	1a5
McCrory John (heirs)		14c4	McCaully J C & E	7W, 1a7
Moore Josiah		14c4	Marshall John S (heirs)	8W, 1a8
Mann Luther		13c3	Martin James	4W, 5W
Malone John ...(Plymouth)	11a7		Meeds James	4W
Moore William	12a7, 14a7		McDonald F	3W
Malone Sarah	11a7, 11a8		Marlow James	1c3
Malone Thomas		11a7	McDermot S G	1c3
Mellick Henry		13a10	Madison John	1c4
May William		10a7	Mannor John	1c5
Morrow D		10a10	McConnell Hugh	1c5, 1c6
McDonough R		15a8	Mitchell Ephraim	1c7
Miller Charles (Sandusky)	10W		Mitchell Robert	1c8
McCully Wm	2a9, 3a9		Millikin John	2c6
Marshall Christian		2a9	Murphey John	2c4
Miller Christian	2c10, 3c10		Marks George	2a7
McCollom Alexander		3c9	Millikin W B	1c7
Martin Jonathan		3c10	Mercer Boyd J	(Troy) 3c8
Meechley Andrew		1c10	Murphey John	3c4
McCully Walter		2a9	Miller David	3c4, 3c5

Name	Ref	Name	Ref
Nisely Daniel	1c10	Patrick J F	12b4
Noble John	15a3	Pettit Isabella (Cass)	15a1
North Guy W	15a7	Pettit Thomas B	14a4
Nimmons James (heirs)	15a7	Pettit Thomas M	14a4
Nimmons M F	15a7	Pettit John	14a4
Nixon R	14a8, 14a9	Pettit Alexander	14a4
Neptune John M	14c3, 14e1	Patterson Sarah	12a3
Norris William	9d4	Paul Andrew	11a3
Norris Susan	10d5	Paul William	10a6
Nesbit David	13d8	Pipher A (Franklin)	6a2
Nichols Jackson	13d5	Pask George	6a2
Osborn Alfred	7b1	Pittenger Abraham	6N
Oberlin John	6s	Powell James	6N
Oberlin S J & Wm	7e1	Powell David	6N
Osborn Ezra	3b5	Powell John	6N
O'Rourk C J	2a4, 3a5	Powell Myers	6N
Ott Conrad	8a5	Peterman John (Jackson)	9a6
Osborn Jacob	1b2	Pittenger J M	6a3, 7a3
Osborn William	4b3, 5b3	Picking C & H	8a5
Osborn Ezra	4b4, 5b4	Powell James	4a3
Osborn Samuel	6b3	Pennybaker R (Jefferson)	9d2
Osborn Alfred	7b2	Patterson Sarah A	9d1
Osborn Charles W	4b4	Palm William	11d3, 12d3
Osborn A	4b2	Platt Charlotte (Madison)	1b1
Oswald J F	8b2, 7b2, 7b3	Painter Andrew	1E, 2E
Oswald Henry	7b2, 7b3	Painter John	1e1
Oswald John	5b2	Pittenger Isaac	3b3
Oswald Benjamin	4d7	Pollock J R	1a2, 2W
Ohler Jacob	5d8	Pittenger J M (Mifflin)	3b5
Overdeer Michael	6a7	Pettit Jonathan	4E
Oswald Jacob	8a10	Patrick David	1d5, 2d5
Orewiler Adam	7a10, 8a10	Peppil George	1d4
Orewiler Eli	6a9	Portner Jesse	1b7
Ozier N & D	11N	Peterson Wm (Monroe)	5d9, 6d9
Olin N G	10c2	Peterson John	3d8, 3d9
Oldfield Richard	10d2, 12d2	Peterson Thomas	4d9
Opdyke Christy	15a4	Parr Andrew	6d9
Opdyke John	15a4	Peterson Solomon	3d9
Opdyke Stacy	14a7, 15a7	Parker Elizabeth (Perry)	1e4
Owings Archabald	10b3	Penn John	14c5
Oberlin Henry	10b3	Poorman Peter	12c5
Oberlin Josiah	10b3, 11b3	Phillips Thomas	10c5
Olin N G	10c3	Painter H	14c3
Olin B F	11c4	Painter George	14c3
Olin Betsey	11c3	Penn Ezekiel C	13c5
Oldfield Abner	13d4	Paste Hannah	11c4
Ottinger Josiah	11d5	Parcello T M (Plymouth)	14a9
O'Harrie James	13d9	Patterson H W	11a7, 12a7, 12a8
Paul Andrew (Bloom'grove)	10b1	Patterson James (heirs)	11a7
Powell William	13b1, 12N	Parcello William	14a9
Powell Henry & James	12b1	Parcello W M	13a9
Pipher Jacob	12a1, 11N	Price Magdalena	12a9
Pittenger Albert	10a1, 10a2	Preston John	14a8
Patterson William (Butler)	14b5	Preston William	13a8
Patterson Robert Sr	14b5, 14b4, 15b4	Patterson David	12a8
Patterson Robert Jr	15b4	Patterson D	12a8
Porcher John	12b1	Paramour M B (Sandusky)	3a9

Post David....... (Sharon).... 8a8	Rose Margret................. 14a3
Post Daniel................... 4a7	Rose A M.................14a3
Paramour M B............... 6a8	Rinehart F (heirs)............ 10a5
Pitts Wm.... (Springfield)...... 3a6	Ralston Jno.... (Franklin).. 7N, 6b1
Paramour John...:........... 2a7	Ralston Robert................7N
Pitts David................. 1a5	Ralston Rebecca.............. 7N
Post Jeremiah................ 4W	Ralston Paul..............5N, 7N
Post Prudence................ 4W	Ralston George................ 6b1
Patterson Robert.............. 1c4	Robinson William............. 5b1
Pletcher Samuel M............ 2c8	Rupert C...................... 9a2
Phillips David................ 2c4	Roush Samuel..... (Jackson)... 7a4
Pile A J...:................. 6W	Roads & Henry........... 9a5, 9a6
Patton George................ 3a5	Roush Abraham............... 7a3
Purdy Archibald............ 3a6, 3a7	Roberts Jesse................. 6a6
Perry Wm........ (Troy.... 8c5, 8c6	Ritenhouse E............ 4a4, 5a3
Post William............... 3c5, 3c6	Roberts David................ 7a6
Post Henry................... 3c6	Rice John F................... 5a6
Proctor James:............... 5c5	Rex George.... (Jefferson).... 10d3
Pool A R.................... 3c6	Robinson Thomas.............. 9d2
Pipher Andrew............... 3c5	Robinson James............... 10d2
Palmer C.... (Washington)..... 3c1	Robinson John Jr............. 10d2
Pollock Thomas............ 5d2, 6d3	Robinson Calvin............ 11s, 12s
Piper George................... 5s	Robinson William............. 12d1
Piper William................ 6s	Rhodes Samuel R............. 11c2
Palm David A............... 7c2	Russell John................. 13d3
Palm James................. 7c2	Richards Isaac............... 13c2
Pearce J M.................. 6d3	Riddle John................. 10d3
Pittenger Mary... (Weller).... 5b3	Race Samuel..... (Madison).... 2d2
Pittenger H S............... 4b3	Rummell John F................ 2s
Pittenger Charles.......... 5b3, 5b4	Raitt James................. 2E
Pittenger H O............... 5b3	Robinson Jane N.............. 2d2
Painter John E.............. 4b4	Reed John.................... 2c2
Pittenger L N............... 4b2	Ross Levi................... 1d3
Piper John... (Worthington) 12d4	Roberts George.............. 3b3
Peeler John F.............. 10d8	Ritter C & M Thrush.......... 3E
Peeler F A & J A..:....... 11d2	Riblet David................ 1d2
Prichard Wm........... 12d7, 12d8	Rummell Lewis............... 2d3
Prichard Edward........... 13d7	Reed Mary..... .... (Mifflin)..... 2b5
Price Mary................. 13d7	Roberts George............ 3b4, 3b5
Parkeson S C............... 10d9	Ross Catherine............. 2d6
Phillips Samuel............. 11d5	Royer F D & Co.............. 2d7
Peeler John F.............. 10d7	Retnan John................. 6E
Prichard John.............. 13d7	Robinson Uriah.... (Monroe)... 6d8
Quinby E.................... 3b6	Ross Catherine.............. 3d8
Quinn Daniel................ 10N	Ruh Caroline................ 5d6
Quinn Mary................. 10N	Ross Natcher................ 6d8
Quinn Samuel............... 10N	Robinson William............ 5d8
Ruth Jacob.... (Bloom'grove) 11a1	Reed Joseph................ 1d8
Rogers Joseph............... 15N	Royer A J.................. 6d9
Ropp Emanuel............... 11b1	Reader John........... 7d5, 7d9
Randall W H................. 11N	Rider Levi R................ 8d5
Richardson M.... (Butler)... 13b2	Rea Eliza................... 8d8
Richardson J M.............. 13b2	Robinson & Wilson........... 3d8
Robinson James............. 13b3	Rider George................ 8d4
Rice John............... 12b2, 13b2	Ruhl John........ (Perry)... 12c4
Rutman Joshua...... (Cass)... 13a5	Ruhl William........ 11c3, 12c3
Ralston Alexander........... 14a6	Ritchie W A................ 9c4

Ruhl Elijah	12e5
Robinson E .... (Plymouth)	15a7
Ruckman Joseph	14a8, 15a8
Ruckman Joshua	14a8, 15a8
Reynolds B	15a7
Rice Michael	11a7
Row Jacob	11a7
Roush William	10a7
Rooks Leonard	15a9, 15a10
Rooks E	15a10
Rogers Daniel	10a10
Ralston James	13a9
Robins O	15a8
Reaster Michael .. (Sandusky)	1a10
Roe Joseph	1c9
Reed J N	1a9, 2a9
Riblet Daniel	9W
Riblet J P K	1c9, 9W
Root John	2c9
Reed Matthew	10W, 1a10
Rogers Almanza.... (Sharon)	7a7
Roberts George	7a7
Roberts Richard	7a7
Roberts David	7a7
Ridgely Ignatius	5a9
Runda Jacob	4a10, 5a10
Runda Matthias	4a10, 5a10
Randall L	5a10
Reynolds William	6a10
Roberts B & O	5a10
Ringer Wm.... (Springfield)	1a6
Ringer Elias	1a6, 2a8
Ralston William	1a6, 1a7
Roe Joseph	1c7, 7W, 8W
Roe Washington	1c8
Rinehart W H	3W
Roseberry J C	4W, 1c4
Rank John	7W
Reed & Underwood	1a4
Read John	2c6
Rank John.... (Troy)	3c8
Ruhl William	3c6
Ritter William .. (Washington)	7d1
Ritter Samuel	5c2
Ritchie William	7d1
Ritchards Alfred	3d1
Rusk John	3c2
Rodocker John	6c1
Ramey Jacob W	6s, 6c1
Remey John J	6d2
Ridenour Jacob	7d3
Ridenour B F	7d3
Ridenour Martin	7d1
Race Samuel F	4d2
Runyon & Balliet.... (Weller)	5b2
Redding Edward	4b2
Rutan Adam	5b3, 5b4

Robinson Thomas (heirs)	5b4
Redrup James	4b3
Runyon E M	4b3
Ross Wm ... (Worthington)	13d5
Ramsey John	11d5, 12d6, 14d8
Reader Adam	12d6
Reader Philip	12d6
Riddle Samuel	10d8
Robinson Benjamin	10d8
Rammel Lewis	9d5
Rummel D J	11d6, 12d6
Rummel Peter	11d8, 12d8
Remey John W	14d5
Remey Jacob	14d5
Roland Hannah	14d6
Reihard J B & C B	9d6, 9d7
Stout George.... (Bloom'grove)	15N
Snapp Peter	11N
Stoner Jacob F	13b1
Stoner Henry	13b1
Schambs George	11a2
Saviers Charles	11b1
Stevenson Duncan	11a2
Sonanstine J	10b1
Sinker John G	10b1
Stack U (heirs)	12a1
Stack Samuel	12a1
Seaton A	11N, 12b1
Starr Mitchell	11b1
Smith Frederick S	11a2, 12a2
Shoup Daniel...... (Butler)	10b5
Stoner J C	14b2, 15b3
Stone Jacob F	13b2
Stone Jacob	13b2, 15b2
Steel Casper	10b2
Scorgie James	15b5
Sellers E C	14b5
Stratton Mary	13b5
Stormlinson Ann	13b4
Stemple Adam	15b3
Sutton James	15b3
Souter James	13b4
Seaton Alexander	11b2, 12b2
Starr Noble	12b2
Starr R Sen	11b2, 12b2
Shearer Philip	14b4
Stevenson John	12b3
Sampsell Jacob	11b2
Smalley David	14b4
Sampsell Peter	11b2
Seehrist George B	10b2
Seehrist Peter	10b2, 10b3
Strimple S C (Cass)	15a4
Scoby Archibald	15a3
Smith Catherine	11a4
Sheely Jacob	11a5
Schambs George	10a3, 11a3

Shaver L B	15a4	Spain John W	9s
Swanger Jacob	12a4	Sites Robert	12c1 13s
Swanger Peter	12a4	Saunders William	13c2
Stevenson Duncan	12a3	Steltz Philip	12d2
Stevenson James	12a3	Swank Casper	13d2
Sander George	12a4	Sweet N B & Curtis	13s, 14c1
Swartz Leonard	11a5, 11a6	Steltz Abraham	13s
Snyder David	10a5, 10a6	Scott S	13s
Shine Adam	10a5	Smith Valentine	13d3
Shemberg & Co	14a6, 15a6	Stuff Jacob	10c2
Shatzer Jeremiah	11a3	Strader Julia	12d3
Stull Francis (Franklin)	9a2	Stafford W J	10d3
Snapp Peter	9N, 9a1	Swander John	14c2
Stoner John M	9a2	Stocking Z S (Madison)	1N
Stoner John sen	5a2	Sonner John P	1b1, 1b2
Shoemaker Margret	5b1	Simmons Joseph	3b1
Snyder Jacob M	4a2	Shull Solomon	3E
Small J W	5a2	Stewart Calvin	3b3
Snarely A	8N	Stewart Mary A	2b3
Sturtz Andrew	8b1	Stewart G	1a2
Stover John (Jackson)	7a5	Stewart John (heirs)	2E
Stump A N & G H	5a6	Smith Mary	3b3
Sutter Samuel	8a6	Smith Thomas	2d3
Swanner John	7a5	Stoutenhour Benjamin	3b1
Shade John G	7a6	Shultz Sanford	2b2
Sheldon Alva	7a6	Stocking Eliza	1N
Shull William	6a6	Sears R & A R	2s
Smith John	6a4	Sturges Dimond	1a1, 1W
Swake John H	6a3	Shortess John	2W
Stock John	5a6	Sturges E	1s, 2s, 1c1
Strock John	4a6	Sears John	2s
Shade Jacob	5a3	Sherman John	1W
Stover John	8a5	Sewell William	1c2
Sprague John	6a5	Smith William	3a1
Shearer John	5a4, 6a3	Sunkle C (Mifflin)	3b5
Spaulding Miles (Jefferson)	9s	Sites Henry	3b4, 3b5
Shafer R A	9s	Snyder Casper	1b6
Strong Solomon	11d1	Shoup George	1b5
Swank Zack	14d3	Swoverland Peter	6E, 1b6
Snyder Sarah	13d1	Simpson Samuel	1d7
Steel John	11c2	Snyder D M	2d4
Shafer Adam	9c1, 9c2	Snyder John	2d4
Shafer Michael	9c1, 9c2	Swartz Abraham	2d4
Shafer John	9c2	Swartz Joseph	2d5
Shafer S C	9c2	Stayman Jacob	1b7
Shafer Samuel	11s, 12s, 11d1	Stayman Henry M	2b7
Shafer James	11c1, 11c2	Sheets Samuel	2d6
Shafer Adam G	11c1, 12c2	Swigart George W (Monroe)	7d5
Shafer George jr	12c2	Shennebarger Susan	3d7
Shafer Henry	12c2	Stambaugh George	3d9
Shafer Benjamin	14c2	Shennebarger Jacob	3d7
Shafer Isaac	13c2	Sackman Henry	3d7
Steel Alexander	9c2, 11c1	Smith David (heirs)	3d6
Steel Henry	9d3	Smart Perry	3d6
Spade William	9d1	Smith John	3d5, 6d9
Smith Jonathan L	11c1	Smith Aaron	3d5
Sechrist H J	10d3	Smart Joseph	3d5

Name	Location
Snyder Daniel	3d4
Switzer Peter	2d5, 3d5
Sackman Henry	4d8
Shennebarger E	5d9
Shrack Charles	7d6, 8d7
Shennebarger R	4d5, 5d5
Smith Levi	5d5
Swan Jesse	4d8, 5d8
Sechrist Samuel	7d4, 8d4
Smith Henry	5d6
Shaffer John	5d6
Switzer Josiah	6d6
Stout Hiram	6d7
Swigart Leonard	7d6, 7d7
Shrack David	7d7, 8d7
Sparks Mahlon	7d4, 8d4
Stewart David	7d4
Stewart William	8d5
Stemely Lydia	8d6
Stoffer Elizabeth	3d9
Swan George	4d8
Swigart George	8d6, 7d6
Stewart Sarah J	7d4
Senate Susan	5d9
Stilwell J C (Perry)	13c3
Shafer Jacob	9c3
Shafer John L	9c3
Shafer Frederick	9c3, 10c3
Shafer George Jr	11c3
Shafer George	12c3
Shafer Michael	9c3
Streby Samuel	10c4
Strome Jonas	10c5
Streby John	9c5
Shively Jacob	9c5
Steel John	11c3
Snyder John (Plymouth)	10a8
Shoup John	11a8, 12a9
Shutt John & Co	15a9
Shutt Susan	15a9
Souder John	11a10
Shaver Margaret	13a8
Snyder Fanny	13a10
Seydel Samuel	15a8
Swope Margaret	15a7
Slaybaugh Jacob (Sandusky)	3a10
Seltzer David	2a10
Scott William	1a9, 1a10
Shull Charles J	1a9
Scot Mary	10W
Stonestreet John	1c10
Stoninger Jacob	1a9
Snyder David	2c10
Stephens Henry	3c10
Sheppard M M	2a10
Sprow Jacob	9W
Schunck Nicholas	1c9
Swineford Philip	1c10
Snyder John	3c9
Shell George	3c9
Slaybaugh George (Sharon)	6a8
Slaybaugh William	8d8
Sipe Daniel	7a9
Stevining Jacob	4a7
Snyder John	8a10
Snyder George W	8a10
Stentz John	6a10, 7a9, 7a10
Simon Mary C	6a9
Sifflin Theobald	5a10
Shile Sanderline	4a9, 4a10
Stone Peter	4a8
Starkely Charles	4a10
Smith Martin	4a9
Smiley Jay	8a7
Sutter Samuel	8a7
Swenney Alex. (Springfield)	2c3
Scott Thomas E	2c4
Sturges Edward	2a8
Sanders Thomas	3a6, 3a8
Stewart Robert	3a5
Sheppard Jane	3a7
Sanders Sarah	3a7
Swords Dennis	1c6
Swards Frank	1c3
Scott Maria	2c6
Steward Edward	2c5
Stewart James	6W
Stafford John M	2a6
Snyder Thomas	3a8
Shiffler John	3a6
Smith Charles J	2a6
Scott George	2a6
Siber Adam	2c7
Shaffer Charles C	2c5
Stewart Jacob (Troy)	5c4, 5c5
Sloan Jonathan	3c3, 4c3
Shaffer Charles	3c5
Scott John	3c4
Straub Jacob	5c5
Shauck Aaron	7c6
Shauck H L	7c6
Shuler Samuel	8c5
Shaffer Jacob	8c3
Smith Thomas (Washington)	3d3
Stone William	4d3, 5d3
Stone Charles	4d3, 5d3
Smith Jedediah	3d3, 4d3
Smith John	5d3
Smith John P	6d1
Stewart John	3d1, 3d2, 4d1
Swishur Samuel E	3d1
Shadel William	3s, 3d1, 4c1
Straul Philip	3s
Sloan T W	4c2

Stoadt John................4s	Snyder John................10d8
Stoadt T W................5s	Strader F.........12d6, 13d6, 14d6
Stoadt J P................5s	Simmons Abraham............11d8
Serples James................4d3	Snyder Jeremiah............13d8
Stroup Michael............5d2, 6d2	Simmons Nathan............11d8
Shoup Solomon..............6d5	Secrist John............11d5
Sell G C................5d3	Sheer Jane................12d5
Shindler Christopher....5d2, 6d1, 6d2	Stotler Adam............12d9
Sonner John A................5d1	Smith Henry (heirs)............12d9
Strader John P................5d1	Stotler Elizabeth........13d8, 13d9
Strader John................5c1	Swendel Arthur............13d8
Strader John W............6s, 6d1	Smith Eunice............9d5
Strader Mary M............5d2	Snyder J D............9d6
Sickinger Jacob............5s, 5d1	Simmons William............13d6
Strausbaugh Peter............6c2	Spohn Martin............13d5
Strausbaugh John........6c2, 7c2	Stoufer John............14d4
Spence Jacob............6d1	Simmons A F............13d4, 14d5
Spayde Samuel............7d3	Shafer J S............14d6
Spayde John............8d1	Sheckler Edward............12d4
Straugh John W............7d1	Strader John............13d6
Shafer J and S............8c2	Stewart William............9d5, 9d6
Sechrist Henry............8d2	Secrist Michael............12d5, 14d9
Sechrist George............8d3	Secrist John............12d5
Sower Jacob............4s, 5c1	Smith Philip............9d5
Spohn Martin............8d1	Thompson T (Bloom'grove) 15N
Swigart John M............5d3, 6d3	Turbet John............13a1, 13a2
Smith William......(Weller)....4b3	Thompson Charles (Butler) 15b4
Saltzgaber Samuel............4b2	Tucker Thomas............14b5, 15b5
Stevenson Samuel............6b3, 6b4	Tyler William............12b5, 13b5
Stevenson Levi............5b5, 6b3	Thompson Samuel............15b2
Stewart Charles............7b3, 8b3	Tucker Noah............14b2
Stevenson W A............7b3	Tomlinson Joseph............14b2
Stentz Bartholomew............7b2	Toman J A (Cass) 15a6
Shreffler Samuel (heirs)............8b3	Taylor F W (Franklin) 5a1
Snavely Abraham............9b3	Throne Michael 4N, 5N
Swineford Anthony............9b5	Taylor Robert............5a1
Swineford Israel............9b5	Tooker George............6a1
Seaton Ambrose............9b5	Taylor Henry......(Jackson) 7a4
Springer Francis............4b4	Tucker William............7a6
Shaffer Jacob (Worthington)..14d6	Terris Wm ....(Jefferson) 9d3
Sturges E sr............9d7, 10d7	Teeter John............9d3, 10d3
Spayd Daniel............9d5, 10d5	Tinkey George............12d1
Secrist Eli............11d5	Tinkey J & J S............11d2
Stotler Henry............14d8	Thompson A G............12d2, 12d3
Shennebarger J............9d6, 9d7	Tidd W & S............13c1
Sharp Hiram............9d6	Turman G & H ...(Madison) 3N
Snavely Joseph............9d4, 9d5	Turman James............2a1, 2N
Smith Henry............9d5	Tingley Thomas............1b1
Secrist D............9d5, 10d5	Tyler Samuel............2b2
Spayd J............9d5	Twitchell Charles............1a1, 2a1
Snyder Peter............9d4	Trimble W S............1a2
Snyder John............9d4	Trimble M M (heirs)............1a2
Secrist J............9d4, 10d4	Trimble David S............2W
Swihart Joshua............10d4	Thompson James............1a2
Snyder Samuel............10d4	Tucker Moses (Monroe) 6d7
Snyder Jacob............10d4	Thompson Joseph............5d4, 6d4
Secrist Michael............10d5, 11d5	Thompson James............6d5

Thompson William	6d4	Urich Isaac	7a8
Tucker Gould	7d8	Vosbinder Ann	3b1
Tucker David	5d4, 6d4	Vonhoff Lewis	1b2
Tucker Andrew	7d6	Vosbinder David 4s, 5s, 4d1, 5d1	
Tarris George	6d5	Vanderbilt Jane	6c2
Thuma Peter (Perry)	9e4	Voegley Henry	4d1
Tucker A J (Plymouth)	15a8	Vandorn Nathan	8s, 8c1
Trauger Jonas	15a8	Vandorn John	8c1
Trauger J	15a9	Vantilburg John	2b5
Trauger S H	15a9	Vinson James	6a4
Trauger Tobias	15a9	Vantilburg Vincent	7b4, 8b4
Tarlton Mary	12a7, 12a8, 11a8	Varnum J C	7c3
Trulove Henry	11a7, 11a8, 12a9	Valentine Rebecca	11a1
Tomlinson S	10a10, 10a11	Vanscoyae G W	15b3
Tomlinson George	13a10	Viers L D	15b4
Taylor Catherine	10a7	Viers Martin H	14b2
Tyson John	15a7	Vaughn Rebecca	12d9
Thrush Jacob (Sandusky)	3a10	Vance John	14d9
Thrush Joseph	2a10	Walker Jos (Bloom'grove)	15b1
Tucker Simeon (Sharon)	8a7	Walker Margaret	14b1
Tucker Benj	5a7, 6a7	Ward Sylvanus	14b1
Taylor Wm (Springfield)	2a6	Walker Jacob (heirs)	11a1
Trimble James S	1a7, 1a8	Wilson Joseph H	15N
Tyler Cyrus	2a8	Wilson Drucilla	15a1
Tyler Joseph	3a5	Wolf John W	15a1
Thuma Fanny (Troy)	8c4	Wilson John	12b1
Thuma Josiah S	5c5	Wolf Daniel	12b1, 13b1
Thuma Wm F	7c4	Whisler Christian	13b1
Thuma Jacob W	7c3, 7c5	Weaver Jacob	12N, 12b1
Thuma John	3c3, 7c4	Witt Elizabeth	11a1
Thornton F & A (Washington)	8c2	Walkup Andrew	10a2
Toby Jacob	5d2, 6d2	Welling Margaret	14N
Toby John J	4d1	Whisler William	11a2
Toby Martin	5d1	White Philip	14b1
Toby John	5d1, 6d1, 6d2	Wolf Daniel (Butler)	12b2
Toby Matthias	5d2	Wood John	13b3, 14b3
Thompson James	4s, 5c1, 6c2	Walker Joseph	15b2
Thompson Wm	6d3	Wharton James	13b5
Thompson Isaac H	6d3, 7d3	Wharton Samuel	12b2
Taylor Robert	5d3	White John	12b4
Thrush George	5d3, 6d3	Wolverton D	12b4
Taylor R Sen	4d2	Wetz Thomas (Cass)	12a4
Tisher Michael	4c2	Wischart Catherine	13a4
Taylor John (Weller)	9b3	Wakefield C W	14a4
Traxler Philip (Worthington)	10d4	Weiser Adam	10a4
Teeter S A	12d5	Willet Wm (heirs) 12a5, 13a6, 14a6	
Teeter David	12d5, 12d6	Willet A Sen 13a6, 14a5, 14a6	
Taylor David	14d4, 14d5	Willet A Jr	12a6
Towns William	9d7, 13d7	Willet A W & J	13a5
Traxler P	11d4	Willet W & T	12a6, 13a6
Urich Joseph (All Townships)	2a1	White Elizabeth	13a5, 14a5
Urich David	6N, 7N	White Milton	14a3
Urich Christian	8b1, 9b1	Weirick Samuel	14a4
Urich Alfred	8b1	Wentz Henry 10a5, 10a6, 11a4, 11a5	
Underwood James	1a3, 3W	Wentz Solomon	11a5
Umbarger Leonard	1c6, 2c6	White Samuel	13a4, 13a5
Urich John	9b3	Wentz David	10a5

Ward William P...... 14a5	Will Valentine.... (Sharon).. 4a8
Wood J C 11a4	Weaver John 5a10, 6a10
Walkup Andrew...... 10a3	Widener Wendall...... 4a7
Wolf John C ...(Franklin) 5b1	Weaver Joseph...... 5a9
Wells George...... 7a1	Watty Balsor...... 5a10
Wagner David...... 8a2	Wentzinger Michael...... 5a10
Whisler Jacob...... 6N, 9a2	Wentz Henry...... 4a9, 4a10
Whitmyer Susan...... 9a2	Walser Joseph...... 5a10
Wolferd William...... 5b1	Wormley Jacob...... 8a8
Whisler Isaac...... 4b1	Wilson Charles...... 8a7
Wareham Wm ...(Jackson)... 7a6	Wilson Edgar...... 9a7
Welsh John...... 4a4	Work James (Springfield) 8w
Weaver Solomon...... 7a3	Welsh John 3a3, 3a4
Wilson Eli...... 8a6	Welsh Joseph 3a3
Weaver D (Jefferson). 9s,10s,10d1	Williams Jacob...... 3a5
Watson Levi...... 10s,12c2	Williams Philip...... 2a6
Welrick John...... 11c1	Williams Robert...... 2a6
Weaver William...... 11c2	Weller Samuel...... 7w
Walker Levi...... 13c1,14c1	Webster Orin.... 1c6
Walker James & B...... 11d1	Wiley William ... 1c6, 2c6
Weaver Jacob...... 10d3	Walker Samuel...... 1c8
Wise Christian (Madison)...1b1	Walker Robert...... 2c6
Winebrenner Catherine...3N	Woods Dorathy...... 1c8
Wise Henry...... 2b2	Woods Andrew 2c6, 2c7
Wise John...... 2a2	Wolf Jacob.... 2c6
Williams Amanda...... 1b3	Wolf Jacob (Troy) 3c6, 3c7
Wallace Cyrus...... 1b2	Wolf John...... 3c7
Wallace Margret...... 1b2	Walker John G.... 4c5
Wiler John...... 1b1	Wert John L 7c4
Wirtz S & M...... 3b2	Winters Michael...... 7c6
Wise Emanuel...... 3a1	Walcot E...... 3c3
Ward Joseph ...(Mifflin)... 5b5	Williams Henry...... 8c5
Woodhouse Joseph...... 1b4	Wells William . 3c8
Watters Hiram...... 5E	Wise Peter...... 8c6
Woodhull W A ...(Monroe). 3d9	Winterstein J...... 8c4
Weirick Henry...... 4d9	Winterstein H...... 8c3
Williams Joseph...... 4d6	Wilson James...... 8c4
Woodhull J S...... 4d9	Wickard G (Washington).. 3d1
Weirick J L...... 4d9	Wagner John...... 6d1, 6d2
Wolf John...... 6d7	Weigle Peter...... 4c1
Wolf Joseph...... 6d7, 7d7, 7d8	Woodruff B F...... 7s
Welty Christian 6d7, 6d8, 7d7	Wilkinson William...... 8s
Wighton T W...... 6d8	Wharton James (Weller) 7b5
Wighton William...... 7d8	Wharton Thomas 9b3, 9b4
Wiles F B...... 6d5	Wharton Ammassa...... 9b4
Walters Moses ...(Perry)... 9c5	Wigley James M...... 4b3
Woodrow John...... 9c5	Wolford George...... 5b2, 5b3
Weirick Peter...... 13c4	Walters David...... 5b2
Walters Mahlon...... 14c4	Ward John . 5b4
Willet Thomas.... (Plymouth). 15a7	Ward Christian.... 9b3, 9b4, 9b5
Willet William (heirs) .13a7,14a7	Williams James 8b5, 9b5
Wheeler Isaac...... 10a8	Wolf Henry 8b5
Webber David B...... 13a9	White Elias (Worthington) 10d5
Witherell Alexander...... 10a7	White S S 10d5
Willet Abraham...... 12a7, 13a7	Watt Noah...... 10d7
Walters George.... (Sandusky) 2a9	Warren William.... 12d4
Wheelhouse Stephen...... 2a10	Wonders Valentine 12d9

Whistler Theodore	13d9	Yookey John 15a3
Wilson Samuel 13d7, 14d7		Young William 12b5
Worley David 13d6		Yearing Thomas M 11d4
Wolford George 12d8		Zelner Jonas 2E
Warner Dutton 14d4		Zackman John 8a2
Wise John 12d4, 13d4		Zackman Jacob 8a2
Weaver John 11d9		Zeiters John 5W, 6W
Young Charles (All Townships) 3E		Zeiters Jacob 9a3
Yearing Peter 3b2		Zediker John 5d6
Young Philip 6e1		Zoda Henry 7d9
Yeaman Robert 7E		Zellner Elizabeth 8d6
Yeaman Joshua 1d7, 7E		Zeigler James 15b1
Young David 2d5, 1d6		Zeigler Benjamin 13N
Yoha Eli 1d6		Zeigler John 13a1
Yeates Joseph 2d7		Zeigler Henry 11b1
Yeager Christian 5d4		Zent George (heirs) 10c2
Yeager John 5a10		Zimmerman Peter 1c10
Young William S 13N		Zeiters David 11a4, 11a5
Young John 12s		Zeigler Henry 11b2
Yeager Daniel 13d3		Zimmerly John 12e5
Yocum John 1e9		Zimmers Jacob & Michael 9c3

THE IMPROVED SUBDIVISIONS OF SECTIONS.

No. 1.

No. 2.

No. 3.

No. 4.

THE SUBDIVISIONS EXPLAINED.

Diagram No. 1 represents a Section in Quarters of 160 acres each. No. 2 and 3 are Quarters divided into 80 acre lots both ways—and No. 4 is a Section divided into 40 acre lots. Any part of a Section is readily described by adding the proper figure to the letter designating the Quarter. Like the *systematic numbers*, the letter *a* is used for North West, *b* North East, *c* South West, and *d* South East.

The importance of these concise and definite descriptions, when used in Tax Duplicates, Tax Receipts and Advertisements, will be seen by the following examples, exhibiting the CONTRAST between the *old* and *new* plan of designating the location of the same pieces of land:

Old.---Range 17, Tp. 22, Sec. 6, N. E. ¼ N. W. qr.   *New.*---Sec. 3d4, a8.
Old.---Range 19, Tp. 22, Sec. 6, N. half N. E. qr.   *New.*---Sec. 9a8, b5.

It will be seen that the *systematic number* of the section designates its precise location without giving either the Range or Township. Section 3d4 is 3 miles south and 4 east from the county seat;—9a8 is 9 north and 8 west. If the owner of a farm wishes to sell it, Sec. 9a8, b5, would fix its location more definitely than to fill up half of his advertisement for that purpose.

THE GOVERNORS OF OHIO, WITH THE TIME EACH SERVED.

Arthur St.Clair,	1788 to 1803	Thomas Corwin,	1840 to 1842
Edward Tiffin,	1803 to 1807	Wilson Shannon,	1842 to 1844
Thomas Kirker, (acting)	1807 to 1807	T. W. Bartley, (acting)	1844 to 1844
Samuel Huntington,	1808 to 1810	Mordecai Bartley,	1844 to 1846
Return J. Meigs,	1810 to 1814	William Bebb,	1846 to 1848
O. Looker, (acting)	1814 to 1814	Seabury Ford,	1848 to 1850
Thomas Worthington,	1814 to 1818	Reuben Wood,	1850 to 1853
Ethan A. Brown,	1818 to 1822	William Medill,	1853 to 1856
Allen Trimble, (acting)	1822 to 1822	Salmon P. Chase,	1856 to 1860
Jeremiah Morrow,	1822 to 1826	William Dennison,	1860 to 1862
Allen Trimble,	1826 to 1830	David Tod,	1862 to 1864
Duncan McArthur,	1830 to 1832	John Brough,	1864 to 1865
Robert Lucas,	1832 to 1836	Cha's Anderson, (ac'g)	1865 to 1866
Joseph Vance,	1836 to 1838	Jacob D. Cox,	1866 to 1868
Wilson Shannon,	1838 to 1840	R. B. Hayes,	1868 to

PRESIDENTS OF THE UNITED STATES.

Names.	Residence.	Term of Service.	Birth.	Death.
George Washington,	Virginia	1789 to 1797	1732	1799
John Adams,	Massachusetts	1797 to 1801	1735	1826
Thomas Jefferson,	Virginia	1801 to 1809	1743	1826
James Madison,	Virginia	1809 to 1817	1751	1837
James Monroe,	Virginia	1817 to 1825	1759	1831
John Q. Adams,	Massachusetts	1825 to 1829	1767	1848
Andrew Jackson,	Tennessee	1829 to 1837	1767	1845
Martin Van Buren,	New York	1837 to 1841	1782	1862
Wm. H. Harrison,	Ohio	1841 to 1841	1773	1841
John Tyler,	Virginia	1841 to 1845	1790	1862
James K. Polk,	Tennessee	1845 to 1849	1795	1849
Zackary Taylor,	Louisania	1849 to 1850	1784	1850
Millard Filmore,	New York	1850 to 1853	1800	
Franklin Pierce,	New Hampshire	1853 to 1857	1801	1869
James Buchanan,	Pennsylvania	1857 to 1861	1791	1868
Abraham Lincoln,	Illinois	1861 to 1865	1809	1865
Andrew Johnson,	Tennessee	1865 to 1869	1808	
Ulysses S. Grant,	Illinois	1869 to	1824	

CHIEF JUSTICES.

John Jay,	New York	1789 to 1795	1745	1829
John Rutledge,	South Carolina	1795 to 1795	1739	1800
Oliver Ellsworth,	Connecticut	1796 to 1801	1752	1807
John Marshall,	Virginia	1801 to 1836	1755	1836
Roger B. Taney,	Maryland	1836 to 1864	1777	1864
Salmon P. Chase,	Ohio	1864 to	1808	

THE TERRITORIES OF THE UNITED STATES.

Territories.	Capitals.	Governors.
Arizona,	Tucson,	R. C. McCormack.
Dacota,	Yancton,	A. J. Faulk.
Idaho,	Boise,	D. W. Ballard.
Indian,	Talequa,	Lewis Downing.
Montana,	Virginia City,	Green C. Smith.
New Mexico,	Santa Fe,	Rob't B. Mitchell.
Utah,	Salt Lake City,	Charles Durkee.
Washington,	Olympia,	Gov. Campbell.
Wyoming,	Cheyenne,	

THE VOTE OF LARGE CITIES FOR PRESIDENT, IN 1868.

Cities.	Seymo'r.	Grant.	Total.
New York, ..	107,669	47,778	155,147
Philadelphia,	58,744	61,262	120,006
Brooklyn, ...	38,031	26,686	64,717
Chicago, ...	17,256	22,425	39,681
Cincinnati,	13,241	18,035	31,276
Baltimore,	21,601	9,052	30,653
St. Louis, ..	13,438	16,136	29,574
Boston, ...	12,235	15,331	27,566
San Francisco,	13,507	12,194	25,701
New Orleans, .	23,897	276	24,173
Buffalo, ...	8,587	9,168	17,755
Newark, N. J.	8,410	9,316	17,726
Pittsburgh, ...	6,462	8,076	14,538
Albany, .	8,138	6,228	14,366
Cleveland, ...	5,739	7,890	13,629
Detroit, ...	6,444	5,908	12,352
Milwaukee,	6,993	4,967	11,960
Rochester,	5,147	5,406	10,553
Louisville,	8,874	1,407	10,281
New Haven, ...	5,505..	3,825	9,330
Troy, ...	4,990	4,305	9,295

Totals,   394,908 295,671 690,579

[The population of a City or State is usualy estimated by multiplying the total vote by a fraction over 6.]

OUR DOMAIN.—The United States and Territories now embrace an area of 3,400,000 square miles. Louisiana and the Mississippi Valley were purchased from France in 1803, for $15,000,000; Florida, from Spain, in 1819, for $3,000,000; Texas was annexed in 1845; California, New Mexico and Utah were purchased from Mexico in 1848, for $15,000,000, and Arazona in 1854, for $10,000.

CHRISTMAS DAY.

The 3d of April, 3d of July, and 2d of October, are always on the same day of the week with Christmas.— These days for the next 33 years, are given below.

S.	M.	T.	W.	T.	F.	S.
1870,	1871,		1872,	1873,	1874,	1875,
....	1876,	1877,	1878,	1879,	....	1880,
1881,	1882,	1883,	...	1884,	1885,	1886,
1887,	....	1888,	1889,	1890,	1891.	....
1892,	1893,	1894,	1895,	....	1896,	1897,
1898,	1899,		1900,	1901,	1902,	1903.

A BUSHEL.—The Winchester Bushel, used in the United States, is a hoop 8 inches deep, $18\frac{1}{2}$ inches in diameter, and contains 2,150.42 cubic inches.

A box 26 by $16\frac{1}{2}$ inches square, & 8 inches deep, will contain a bushel.

A box 12 by $11\frac{1}{2}$ inches square, and 8 inches deep, will contain half a bushel.

A box 8 by $8\frac{1}{2}$ inches square, and 8 inches deep, will contain one peck.

A box 8 by 8 inches square, and $4\frac{1}{2}$ inches deep, will contain one gallon.

A box 7 by 8 inches square, and $4\frac{1}{8}$ inches deep, contains half a gallon.

A box 4 by 4 inches square, and $4\frac{1}{4}$ inches deep, will contain one quart.

BUSHEL WEIGHTS.

The following weights per bushel, have been adopted by the Cincinnati Chamber of Commerce. A few will vary a little from the bushel weights in New York and other markets.

Apples, (dried,)	25
Barley,	48
Barley Malt,	...34
Beans, ...	60
Bluegrass seed, ..	14
Bran,	20
Buckwheat,	52
Canary seed,	60
Charcoal,	30
Clover seed, ...	62
Coal, (Mineral,)	80
Coke, ...	32
Corn meal,	50
Corn,	56
Corn, (in ear,)	70
Flax seed,	56
Hemp seed,	44
Hominy, ...	60
Millet seed, ...	50
Oats,	33
Onions,	56
Onion sets,	25
Peaches, (dried,) ...	...33
Peas, ...	60
Potatoes, ...	60
" (Sweet),	55
Rye, ...	56
Rye Malt, ...	40
Salt, ...	50
Timothy seed,	45
Turnips, ...	..60
Wheat, ...	60

Miles via Rail Roads from Mansfield.

B. & O. Rail Road.
NORTH.

Shelby,	12	Nevada,	33
Plymouth,	20	Up'r Sandusky,	41
Centreville,	27	Lima,	85
Havanna,	31	Delphos.	99
Pontiac,	35	Van Wert,	112
Monroeville,	39	Ft. Wayne,	144
Sandusky City,	54	Columbia,	163
Toledo, via Mon-		Warsaw,	184
roeville,	92	Plymouth,	208
Adrian,	124	Valparaiso,	248
Detroit,	157	Chicago,	292
South Bend,	249	Rock Island,	501
Chicago,	335	Iowa City,	561
SOUTH.		St. Louis,	606
Lexington,	9	Council Bluffs,	807

Belleville,	14	**A.G.W. Rail Road.**	
Independence	20	EAST.	
Ankneytown,	25	Windsor,	8
Fredericktown,	30	Ashland,	17
Mount Vernon,	37	Polk,	25
Utica.	48	West Salem,	30
Louisville,	53	Bridgeport,	37
Varnatta,	56	Seville,	45
Newark,	62	Wadsworth,	51
Wheeling,	170	New Portage,	58
Baltimore,	541	Akron,	65
Washington,	563	C & P Crossing,	78
		Ravenna,	81
P. Ft. W. & C. R. R.		Braceville,	98
EAST.		Warren,	105
Lucas.	7	Erie & P'g Cr'g	134
Perrysville,	14	Evensburg,	152
Loudonville,	19	Meadville,	164
Lakeville,	25	Venango,	175
Shreve,	31	Cambridge,	178
Wooster,	40	Union,	194
Orrville,	51	Concord,	200
Lawrence,	58	Corry,	205
Massillon,	65	Panama,	219
Canton,	73	Jamestown,	232
Alliance,	92	Randolph,	249
Salem,	105	Salamanca,	269
New Brighton,	147	New York,	684
Economy,	158	WEST.	
Pittsburgh,	176	Ontario,	7
Harrisburg,	425	Gailon,	15
Philadelphia,	528	Caledonia,	26
Baltimore,	507	Marion,	36
Washington,	547	Burwick,	41
New York,	618	Richwood,	50
WEST.		Urbana,	84
		Springfield,	97
Crestline,	13	Dayton,	119
Bucyrus,	26	Cincinnati,	179

RATES OF POSTAGE.

Letters, half ounce each.... ...3 cts.
Newspapers, every 13 numbers, 5 "
Periodicals, each number, ...1 "
Books, every 4 ounces. .4 "
  Other Matter, including Pamphlets, Transient Newspapers, Book Manuscripts, and Proof Sheets, with or without corrections, Maps, Prints, Engravings, Sheet Music, Blanks, Paper, Seeds, Cuttings, Roots, &c., 2 cts. for every 4 ounces.
  Weekly Newspapers to subscribers in the county where published, *free.*

To Compute Interest.—One of the best rules for computing interest is to divide the principal by 6, which gives the interest at 6 per centum for one day, with mills under dollars. The interest for one day, multiplied by the number of days required, will give the interest for the time. To multiply the principal by the required days, and divide by 6, will give the same result.

Dividing the principal by 6, will also give the interest for ten days, with cents under dollars, and for 100 days, with mills under cents.

Another Rule.—To obtain 6 per cent for any number of months and days, multiply half the principal by the number of months and one third of the days.

[This rule, like most of those in general use, allows 30 days for one month, and 360, instead of 365, for a year; but it is sufficiently accurate for ordinary business transactions.]

On large sums, the interest for a single day is of great importance.— Six per cent. on our national debt, which was reported on December 1st, 1869, to be $2,648,234,682, for one day would amount to $441,372 44.7, and for ten days, to $4,413,734 47.0.

After computing the interest at 6 per cent. if 7 per cent. is required, add one-sixth; for 8, ¼; 9, ⅓; 10, ⅔.

To Estimate Acres.—To find the acres in a field, multiply the rods long by the rods wide, and divide by 160. An acre contains 160 rods, 4,840 yards, and 43,560 feet.

To Measure a Tree.—To tell if a standing tree will make a stick of timber of the required length, measure from the root of the tree, on the ground, the length of the timber required, and place a stake, the top of which is to be as high as the stump when the tree is cut down : then place another stake five feet nearer the tree, extending five feet higher than the first one. By sighting over the top of the two stakes, the place where the eye strikes the tree will be the length of the stick required.

The following items are copied from the Cincinnati Enquirer Almanac.

A Mile Measure.—A standard English mile, which is the measure that we use, is 5,280 feet in length, 1,-760 yards, or 320 rods. A strip one rod wide, and one mile long, is 2 acres. By this it is easy to calculate the quantity of land taken by roads, and also how much is wasted by fences.

The following table shows the length of miles in different countries, compared with the English mile:

	Miles.	Yards.
Scottish (ancient).	1	224
Irish (ancient)	1	480
German (short)	3	1,570
German (long)	5	1,326
Hanoverian	6	999
Tuscan	1	48
Russian	4	1,197
Danish	4	1,204
Danzic	4	1,434
Hungarian	5	313
Swiss	5	353
Swedish	6	1,140
Arabian	1	360

Roman (modern), 132 yards less than the English mile.

A League Measure.

	Miles.	Yards.
English league.	3	
French league	8	
French posting league	2	743
Spanish judicial league	2	1,115
Spanish common league	5	376
Portugal league	3	1,480
Flanders league	3	1,584

Grain Measure in Bulk.—Multiply the width and length of the pile together, and that product by the height, and divide by 2,150, and you have the contents in bushels.

If you wish the contents of a pile of ears of corn or roots, in heaped bushels, ascertain the cubic inches, and divide by 2,818.

A Ton.—A ton weight, is 2,000 lbs A ton of round timber is 40 cubic feet : of square timber, 54 cubic feet.. A ton of liquid measure is 252 gallons.

A Firkin of butter is 56 lbs.; a tub of butter is 84 lbs.

The Stone Weight, so often spoken of in English measure, is 14 lbs., when weighing wool, feathers, hay, etc., but a stone of beef, fish, butter, cheese, ect., is only 8 lbs.

"A Sabbath day's journey," 1,155 yards, which is 18 yards less than two thirds of a mile.

"A day's journey," 33½ miles.

"A reed," 10 feet, 11⅜ inches.

"A palm," 3 inches.

"A fathom," 6 feet.

A Greek foot is 12½ inches.

A Hebrew foot is 1.212 of an English foot.

A cubit is 2 feet.

A great cubit is 11 feet.

An Egyptian cubit is 21.888 inches.

A span is 10.944 inches.

A Turkish bein, is 1 mile, 66 yards.

Board Measure.—Boards are sold by superficial measure, at so much per foot of one inch or less in thickness, adding one fourth to the price for each quarter inch thickness over an inch.

A PICTURE OF OHIO ONE HUNDRED YEARS AGO.

Col. JAMES SMITH, who was captured by Ohio Indians in 1755, gives in his Journal, published in 1799, a detailed account of his captivity, the ceremonies connected with his adoption into an Indian tribe, and his sojourn with his savage companions in what was then a vast wilderness, but now the highly cultivated and densely populated State of Ohio, which is so interesting that we have concluded to republish portions of the narrative.

After the return of Mr. Smith from Indian captivity, in 1759, he was entrusted with the command of a company of riflemen in Pennsylvania. He trained his men in Indian tactics and discipline, and distinguished himself as an officer both before and during the war of the Revolution. The latter part of his life was spent in Kentucky, where he served for several terms in the state legislature, was much respected, and died in 1812.

HIS CAPTURE.

In the spring of 1755, James Smith, then eighteen years of age, was captured by Indians near Bedford, in Pennsylvania. His captors first led him to the banks of the Alleghany, opposite Fort Du Quesne, where he was compelled to run the gauntlet between two long ranks of Indians placed two or three rods apart. After running some distance without serious injury, he was felled by a blow from a stick or tomahawk handle, and, on attempting to rise, was blinded by sand thrown in his eyes and rendered insensible by repeated blows. When he recovered his consciousness, he found himself within the fort, much bruised, and under the care of a French physician.

A few days afterwards, he was placed in a canoe and taken to an Indian village about forty miles up the Alleghany river, where he remained a few weeks. His captors then took him to the Indian village of Tullihas, on a branch of the Muskingum, near the junction of the Owlcreek with Mohican river, in what is now Coshocton county, Ohio.

HIS ADOPTION BY THE INDIANS.

The ceremonies connected with Smith's adoption by the Indians, while at Tullihas, we give in his own language:

"The day after my arrival at the aforesaid town, a number of Indians collected about me, and one of them began to pull the hair out of my head. He had some ashes on a piece of bark, in which he frequently dipped his fingers, in order to take the firmer hold, and so he went on, as if he had been plucking a turkey, until he had all of the hair clean out of my head, except a small spot about three or four inches square on my crown. This they cut off with a pair of scissors, excepting three locks, which they dressed up in their own mode. Two of these they wrapped with a narrow braided garter, made by themselves for that purpose, and the other they plaited at full length, and then stuck it full of silver brooches. After this they bored

[Continued on alternate pages.]

TABLE *giving the number of days from any day in one month to the same day in any other.*

FROM	Jan.	Feb.	Mar.	Ap.	May.	Jn.	Jul.	Aug.	Sep.	Oct.	Nov.	Dec
January	365	31	59	90	120	151	181	212	243	273	304	334
February	334	365	28	59	89	120	150	181	212	242	273	303
March....	306	337	365	31	61	92	122	153	184	214	245	275
April.......	275	306	334	365	30	61	91	122	153	183	214	244
May	245	276	304	335	365	31	61	92	123	153	184	214
June	214	245	273	304	334	365	30	61	92	122	153	183
July	184	215	243	274	304	335	365	31	62	92	123	155
August......	153	184	212	243	273	304	334	365	31	61	92	122
September...	122	153	181	212	242	273	304	334	365	30	61	91
October ..	92	123	151	182	211	243	273	304	335	365	31	61
November	61	92	120	151	181	212	242	273	304	334	365	30
December .	31	62	90	121	151	182	212	243	274	304	335	365

EXPLANATION.—The number of days from any day of one month to the same day of any other, is found opposite the one and under the other month.

TABLE *showing what Pork should be worth per pound, at different prices per bushel for Corn. The prices are cents.*

Corn.	Pork.	Corn..	Pork.
12½	1.50	38	4.52
15	1.78	40	4.76
17	2.	42	5.
20	2.38	45	5.35
22	2.62	50	5.95
25	2.96	55	6.54
30	3.75	60	7.14
33	3.92	65	7.74
35	4.16	70	8.57

As one bushel of corn is expected to produce 8.40 lbs. of pork, a farmer can ascertain by dividing the price of a bushel of corn by 8.40, whether it is most profitable to sell his corn before or after it is reduced to pork.

THE SIZES OF BOOKS.

The various sized pages of books were named from the number of folds given to a sheet of the largest sized paper then made, which was 19 by 24 inches, as follows:

	Folds.	Leaves.	Pages.
2fo or folio	1	2	4
4to. or quarto	2	4	8
8vo. or octavo	4	8	16
12mo	6	12	24
16mo	8	16	32
18mo	9	18	36
24mo	12	24	48
32mo	16	32	64

Afterwards, when larger sheets of paper were manufactured, books continued to be designated in the same way, but were distinguished from the above by prefixing the name of the sheet. Thus: a sheet 22 by 28 inches, was called "Royal," and books printed on it were called royal folio, royal quarto, royal octa. etc.

TABLE, *showing the comparative difference between good hay, and other articles of food for stock.*

10 lbs. of good hay are equal to
8 to 10 lbs. clover hay,
45 to 50 " green clover,
40 to 50 " wheat straw,
20 to 40 " barley or oat straw,
20 to 25 " potatoes,
25 to 40 " carrots,
30 to 35 " mangold wurtzel,
45 to 50 " turnips,
20 to 30 " cabbage,
3 to 5 " peas and beans,
5 to 6 " wheat and barley,
4 to 7 " oats and corn,
2 to 4 " oil cake.

In the use of the above table much will depend upon the quality of the sample, and the form in which the food is administered. Much also depends upon a change of food and the condition of the animal.

The results of numerous experiments, reported by Agricultural Associations, show, that each 100 lbs. of live weight of the animal, requires of hay or its equivalent, daily, if a horse, 3.08 lbs.—if an ox, 2.40 lbs.

my nose and ears, and fixed me off with ear-rings and nose-jewels. Then they ordered me to strip off my clothes and put on a breech-clout, which I did. They then painted my head, face and body, in various colors. They put a large belt of wampum on my neck, and silver bands on my hands and right arm; and so an old Chief led me out on the street, and gave the alarm halloo, *coo-wigh*, several times, repeated quick; and on this, all that were in the town came running and stood round the Chief, who held me by the hand in the midst. As I at that time knew nothing of their mode of adoption, and had seen them put to death all they had taken alive, I made no doubt but they were about putting me to death in some cruel manner. The old Chief, holding me by the hand, made a long speech, very loud, and when he had done, he handed me to three young squaws, who led me by the hand down the bank, into the river, until the water was up to our middle. The squaws then made signs to me to plunge myself into the water, but I did not understand them. I thought the result of the council was that I should be drowned, and that these young ladies were to be my executioners. They all laid violent hold of me, and I for some time opposed them with all my might, which occasioned loud laughter by the multitude that were on the bank of the river. At length one of the squaws made out to speak a little English (for I believe they began to be afraid of me) and said "*no hurt you.*" I then gave myself up to their ladyships, who were as good as their word; for though they plunged me under water, and washed and rubbed me severely, yet I could not say they hurt me much."

These young ladies then led Smith up to the council house, where some of the tribe dressed him with new clothes and ornaments. They then seated him upon a bear-skin and furnished him with a pipe and tobacco. The Indians then came in, took their seats and remained smoking for some time in profound silence. At length one of the chiefs arose and delivered the following speech, which was communicated to Smith through an interpreter:

"My son, you are now flesh of our flesh and bone of our bone. By the ceremony which was performed this day, every drop of white blood was washed out of your veins; you are taken into the Caughnewago nation and initiated into a war-like tribe; you are adopted into a great family, and now received with great seriousness and solemnity in the room and place of a great man. After what has passed this day, you are now one of us by an old and strong law and custom. My son, you have now nothing to fear: We are now under the same obligations to love, support and defend you, that we are to love and defend one another: therefore, you are to consider yourself as one of our people."

Knowing that the white blood was not washed out of him, Smith did not at the time believe the chief to be sincere in his professions of friendship and fidelity, but states, that while he remained with them, they always

The Old Reliable City and Custom
Boot & Shoe Store.

D. BILLOW & CO.,
SHELBY, OHIO.

The finest, best and cheapest assortment of Boots and Shoes in the country, are to be had at the old reliable Boot and Shoe Store of

D. BILLOW & CO.

They keep on hand and manufacture to order

LADIES', GENTLEMEN'S AND CHILDREN'S WEAR,

of superior make, and at most reasonable prices. Latest styles,

Gaiters, for Ladies and Misses

Men's and Boys' Calf-skin Boots, and
SHOES OF EVERY DESCRIPTION,

They know how to make, buy and sell, and it is the place to get the worth of your money.   D. BILLOW & CO.

Emminger's Grocery!
FOURTH STREET, EAST OF MAIN, MANSFIELD.

Farmers will find it to their interest to call at the above Provision Store before selling elsewhere, as we will give the highest price for all Country Produce. Groceries sold as cheap as any house in the city.

treated him as an equal. Whether clothing and provisions were plenty or scant, all shared alike.

After this part of the ceremonies were completed, Smith was introduced to his new kin, and told that he was to attend a feast that evening. He was accordingly furnished, like the rest, with a bowl and wooden spoon, which each carried with him to the feast. As every one advanced to some brass kettles filled with boiled venison and green corn, he had his share given him, and after one of the chiefs had made a short speech, all began to eat.

The next day a chief, named Pluggy, with a party of warriors, were to start to the frontiers of Virginia. The war dance and war songs, were next to be performed. Those going to war assembled. An old Indian began to sing, timing his music by beating with one stick upon a sort of hollow gum, which made a sound similar to a muffled drum. Each warrior had a tomahawk, spear, or war-mallet in his hand, and they all moved regularly toward the east, or the way they intended to go to war. At length they all stretched their tomahawks toward the Potomac, and giving a hideous yell, they wheeled quick about, and danced in the same manner back. In performing their war songs, only one sings at a time, in a moving posture, with a tomahawk in his hand, while the rest of the warriors are constantly repeating *he uh, he uh*, till the song is ended.

On the next evening Smith was invited to a kind of promiscuous dance. The young men and young women stood in separate ranks, about one rod apart, facing each other. Both men and women sing as they advance towards each other, and, when near enough, stoop till their heads touch—then cease their dancing, and with loud shouts, retreat and form again. The same thing is repeated over and over, for three or four hours, without intermission. In singing, their *ya ne no hoo wa ne* is like our *fa sol la;* and although they have no such thing as jingling verse, they can intermix sentences with their notes, and carry on their tune in concert. This is considered a sort of wooing or courting dance. As they advance, stooping their heads together, they can say what they please to each other, without disconcerting their rough music, or letting others know what is said.

Smith describes an expedition to a buffalo lick, supposed to be in Licking county, where the Indians killed several buffalos, while the squaws, in their small brass kettles, made about half a bushel of salt. In October, he accompanied his adopted brother, whose name was Tontileaugo, to a Wyandot camp, supposed to have been located at or near the mouth of Black River, on Lake Erie. From the description he gives of the country through which they travelled in reaching this camp, they must have passed through what are now parts of Knox, Richland, Ashland and Lorain counties. On arriving, they were kindly received, and here Tontileaugo, who had married a Wyandot woman, found his wife. Among the eatables furnished them was a kind of brown potatoes, which grew spontaneously, and when peeled and dipped in raccoon fat, tasted, Smith says, nearly like our sweet potatoes.

500 Men Wanted!

Unable to supply the unprecedented demand for his

IMPROVED MAPS,

The undersigned can give profitable employment to at least

FIVE HUNDRED GOOD MEN.

Each one assisting in the enterprise, will have charge of certain territory, and be allowed an interest in the proceeds, which shall be proportionate to the capital and labor by him employed. Any man of ordinary business qualifications, can double all the money he will be required to invest, every two months. **Call on him or his agent, at the office of Carpenter & Gass, Mansfield, Ohio.**   JOHN B. MEREDITH.

THE GREAT MAP IMPROVEMENTS.

Editors of newspapers all over the country have referred to the new system of maps in language similar to the following, which is copied from the Richland County Gazette:

THE IMPROVED MAPS.—Hon. JOHN B. MEREDITH, a practical printer, and late Judge of the Probate Court of this county, has secured the copyright for a new system of maps, embracing improvements of such immense value, that it is predicted he will revolutionize, if not control, the entire map business of the country. We have secured a copy of the one he has just published for this county. It is certainly the most practical and useful map we have ever examined. We will not attempt a definite description of the improvements which distinguish his maps from all others. They must be seen to be properly appreciated. An idea of their importance, may be inferred from the fact that more practical information can be obtained from the map before us in one minute, than could be gathered in an hour from those heretofore in use. The miles and course not only to the residence of a person, or to any section of land in the county, but to each county seat of the State and all the principal cities of the United States, are seen at a glance. In addition to its double value as a county map, it supplies the place to a great extent, of one both for the state and nation. Every sensible man will be anxious to secure a copy.

To supply the demand for county maps alone, Judge Meredith will be compelled either to sell the right to publish them, or secure the assistance of a great many active men in each State. As the copyright does away with all competition, and is estimated to be worth more money than any one man could enjoy, he can afford to divide the profits with all who aid him in the work, allowing each to make a fortune. Success to the enterprise.

After giving accounts of several hunts with the Wyandots in the vicinity of the lake, Smith describes another hunting expedition with them up the river. They all embarked in a birch bark canoe, which was about 35 feet long, 4 wide, and 3 deep. Although capable of carrying a heavy burden, it was so light and ingeniously constructed, that four men could carry it for miles. On reaching a good place to hunt, they carried it up the bank, and by turning it upside down, converted it into a house or camp. They kept moving and hunting up the river until they came to the falls, where they remained for several weeks and killed a number of deer, several bears and a great many raccoons. Before leaving this camp, they buried their canoe in the ground, to preserve it during the winter season. After travelling an easterly course about twenty-two miles, they came to a large creek, where their cabin for winter quarters was erected. In building it, they cut logs about fifteen feet long, and placing one upon another, between posts driven in the ground at each end, two walls were erected about twelve feet apart, and four feet high. The posts were tied together with bark. Between these walls, at each end, they placed a fork in the ground, and a large pole extending from one fork to the other, with smaller ones from it to the walls, supported a bark roof. The ends of the cabin were enclosed with split timber, set on end, and the cracks stopped with moss. A bear skin, hung at each end, served as doors, and an opening along the center of the roof, supplied the place of a chimney. In this little hut, 12 by 14 feet square, the whole party, consisting of eight hunters and thirteen squaws, besides boys and children, slept soundly upon their best bedding, consisting of bear skins spread upon brush and linn bark.

Soon after their winter quarters were completed, four of the hunters started upon an expedition against the English settlements, leaving Tontileango, three other Indians and Smith, to supply the camp with food.— The winter months passed in hunting excursions—the bear, even more than the deer, being an object of active and successful pursuit.

In February and March, 1756, while the men and boys were hunting and trapping, the squaws made sugar. They caught and gathered the sugar-water in vessels which they constructed for that purpose out of linn bark. Smith says, "The way we commonly used our sugar when encamped, was by putting it in bear's fat, until the fat was almost as sweet as the sugar itself, and in this we dipped our roasted venison."

In the latter part of March, the squaws having renderd the bears' fat, and placed it in vessels which they had made of deer skins to hold it, the party commenced their return trip. After reaching the Falls and building another canoe of elm bark, they embarked, and reached their camp at the mouth of the river in time to prepare for planting corn. The work, except hunting, trapping, etc., is always performed by the squaws.

On one occasion, after the Indians had given French traders skins for clothing and other necessary articles, Smith describes a visit, in company

with others to the cornfield, where the squaws were at work, as follows :
" After I had got my new clothes, and my head done off like a redheaded
woodpecker, I, in company with a number of young Indians, went down
to the cornfield, to see the squaws at work. When we came there, they
asked me to take a hoe, which I did, and hoed for some time. The squaws
applauded me as a good hand at the business ; but when I returned to the
town, the old men hearing of what I had done, chid me, and said that I was
adopted in place of a great man, and must not hoe corn like a squaw. They
never had occasion to reprove me for anything like this again ; as I never
was extremely fond of work, I readily complied with their orders."

As the Indians, on their return from a winter hunt, bring with them
large quantities of bear's oil, sugar and dried venison, they for a time have
plenty, and do not spare eating or giving. In this way they make way
with their provisions as soon as possible. Having no such thing as regular
meals, if any one would go to the same house several times in a day, he would
be invited to eat of the best—and with them it is bad manners to refuse to
eat when it is offered, being interpreted as a symptom of displeasure.

While provisions were plenty, the hunters became lazy, and spent their
time in singing and dancing, or some other amusement. They appeared
to be fulfilling the scriptures beyond those who professed to believe them,
in that of taking no thought of to-morrow—living in love and peace with
each other. In this respect they shame those who profess Christianity.

The size of this volume forbids the idea of our attempting to notice all the
hunting expeditions and adventures of this Ohio Crusoe, during his captivity of over four years among the Indians. Only that part of his narrative
deemed most interesting to the people of this State, has been referred to.
Should it enable the reader to form a correct idea of the contrast between
"Ohio over one hundred years ago," and its present condition, our object
in noticing Smith and his captors, may be considered accomplished.

———————

MEASUREMENT OF HAY.—The weight of a load of hay taken out of a mow
or old stack, may be ascertained by multiplying the length of the load in
yards by the width in yards, and that by the height in yards, and divide
the product by 20 ; the quotient will be the number of tons.

THE PRICE OF HAY.—An easy mode of arriving at the value of a given
number of lbs. of hay, or anything else sold by the ton of 2000 lbs., is to
multiply the number of pounds by half the price per ton, pointing off three
figures from the right. The remaining figures will be the price.

The principle in this rule is the same as in interest. Dividing the price
by two, gives the price of half a ton, or 1000 lbs ; and pointing off three
figures on the right is dividing by 1000.

TO MEASURE SQUARE TIMBER.—Multiply the breadth in inches by the
depth in inches, and that by the length in feet, and divide the product by
144. The quotient will be the contents in cubic feet.

ORGANIZATION AND SETTLEMENT OF RICHLAND COUNTY.

RICHLAND COUNTY was organized March 1, 1813, and embraced territory 30 miles square. By the erection of the county of Ashland in 1845, and Morrow county in 1848, her boundaries have been reduced to their present limits. A large proportion of the early settlers of the county emigrated from Pennsylvania and Virginia, who commenced settling on branches of the Mohican as early as 1809. Among these pioneers were James McCluer, Samuel McCluer, Henry McCart, Andrew Craig, James Cunningham, Frederick Herring, Abraham Baughman, Henry Nail, Samuel Lewis, Peter Kinney, Calvin Hill, John Murphy, Thomas Coulter, Melzar Tannehill, Isaac Martin, Stephen Van Schoick and Archibald Gardner.

Mansfield was laid out in 1808, by James Hedges, Jacob Newman and Joseph H. Larwill. The last named gentleman pitched his tent on the rise of ground above the Big Spring, and opened the first sale of lots on the 8th of October. The county was then a wilderness, without a road through it. The first purchasers came in from Knox, Columbiana, Stark and other partially settled counties. Among the first settlers of Mansfield were Geo. Coffinberry, Winn Winship, Rollin Weldon, J. C. Gilkison, John Wallace, and Joseph Middleton.

Most of the following facts, derived from Mr. Henry Nail and other early settlers, were published some years since, in Howe's History of Ohio. We have made some corrections and added further particulars.

In September, 1812, shortly after the breaking out of the late war with Great Britain, two block-houses were built in Mansfield. One stood a little south of the center, and the other near the west side of the public square. The first was built by a company commanded by Capt. Shaeffer, from Fairfield county, and the other by the company of Col. Charles Williams, of Coshocton. A garrison was stationed at the place, until after the battle of the Thames.

At the commencement of hostilities, there was a settlement of friendly Indians of the Delaware tribe, at a place called Greentown, within the present township of Green, in Ashland county. This Indian village contained some 60 cabins, with a council-house about 60 feet long, 25 wide, one story in height, built of posts and clapboarded. The village contained several hundred persons. As a measure of safety, they were collected, in August, 1812, and sent to some place in the western part of the state, under protection of the government. They were first brought to Mansfield, and placed under guard, at the run, south-west of the public square. While there, a young Indian and squaw came up to the block-house, with a request to the chaplain, Rev. James Smith of Mt. Vernon, to marry them after the manner of the whites. In the absence of the guard, who had came up to witness the ceremony, an old Indian and his daughter, aged about 12 years, who were from Indiana, took advantage of the circumstance and escaped

Two spies from Coshocton, named Morrison and McColloch, met them near the run, about a mile north-west of Mansfield; and as the commanding officer, Col. Kratzer, had given orders to shoot all Indians found out of the bounds of the place, under the impressson that all such must be enemies, Morrison, on discovering them, shot the father through the breast. He fell mortally wouned—then springing up, ran about 200 yards, and fell to rise no more. The girl escaped.

There was living at this time, on the Black Fork of Mohican, about half a mile west of where Petersburg now is, a Mr. Martin Ruffner. Having removed his family for safety, no person was with him in the cabin, excepting a bound boy. About two miles south-east of Ruffner's house, stood the cabin of the Seymours. This family consisted of the parents—both very old people—a maiden daughter, Catherine, and her brother Philip, who was a bachelor.

One evening Mr. Ruffner sent out the lad to the creek bottom, to bring home the cows, when he discovered four Indians and ran. They called to him, saying they would not harm him, but wished to speak to him. Having ascertained from him that the Seymours were at home, they left, and he hurried back and told Ruffner of the circumstance; upon which he took down his rifle and started for Seymour's. He arrived there, and was advising young Seymour to go to the cabin of Mr. Copus, and get old Mr. Copus and his son to come up and help take the Indians prisoners, when the latter were seen approaching. Upon this, young Seymour passed out of the back door and hurried to Copus's, while the Indians entered the front door with their rifles in hand.

The Seymours received them with an apparent cordiality, and the daughter spread the table. The Indans, however, did not appear to be inclined to eat, but soon arose and commenced the attack. Ruffner, who was a powerful man, made a desperate resistance. Using his rifle as a club, he broke the stock to pieces; but he fell before superior numbers, and was afterwards found dead and scalped in the yard, with two rifle balls through him, and several fingers cut off by a tomahawk. The old people and daughter were found tomahawked and scalped in the house.

In an hour or so after dark, young Seymour returned with Mr. Copus and son, making their way through the woods by the light of a hickory bark torch. Approaching the cabin, they found all dark and silent within. Young Seymour attempted to open the door, when it flew back. Reaching forward, he touched the corpse of the old man, and exclaimed in tones of anguish, "here is the blood of my poor father!" Before they reached the place, they heard the Indians whistling on their powder chargers, upon which they put out the light and were not molested.

These murders, supposed to have been committed by some of the Greentown Indians, spread terror among the settlers, who immediately fortified their cabins and erected several block-houses. Among them was Nail's, on the Clear fork of Mohican; Beam's on the Rocky fork; one on the site of Ganges, and a picketed house on the farm of Thomas Coulter, near the present village of Perrysville, on the Black fork.

Shortly after this, a party of 12 or 14 militia from Guernsey county, who were out on a scout, without any authority burnt the Indian village of Greentown, which at that time was deserted. At night they stopped at the cabin of Mr. Copus, on the Black fork, about 9 miles southeast of Mansfield. The next morning, as four of them were at the spring washing, a few rods from the cabin, they were fired upon by a party of Indians in ambush. They all ran for the house, except Warnock, who retreated in another direction, and was afterwards found dead in the woods, about a half mile distant. His body was resting against a tree, with his handkerchief stuffed in the wound in his bowels. Two of the others, George Shipley and John Tedrick, were killed and scalped between the spring and the house. The fourth man, Robert Dye, in passing between the shed and cabin, suddenly met a warrior with his uplifted tomahawk. He dodged and escaped into the house, carrying with him a bullet in his thigh.

Mr. Copus at the first alarm had opened the door, and was mortally wounded by a rifle ball in his breast. He was laid on the bed, and in a few minutes the Indians attacked the cabin. "Fight and save my family," said he, "for I am a dead man." The attack was fiercely made, and several balls came through the door, upon which they pulled up the puncheons from the floor and placed them against it. Mrs. Copus and her daughter went up into the loft for safety, and the latter was slightly wounded in the thigh, from a ball thrown from a neighboring hill. One of the soldiers, George Launtz, was in the act of removing a chunk of wood from between the logs of the cabin, to make an opening to fire through, when a ball entered the hole and broke his arm. After this, he watched till he saw an Inian put his head from behind a stump, when he fired, and the fellow's brains were scattered over it. After about an hour, the Indians having suffered severe loss, retreated. Had they first attacked the house, it is probable that the Indians would have gained an easy victory.

It is proper to state that there are several versions of this skirmish at the cabin of Mr. Copus. The oldest settlers do not agree in several particulars. In a note appended to the above account, as narrated by Mr. Howe, he says, " We have three different accounts of this affair: one from Wyatt Hutchinson, of Guernsey, then a lieutenant in the Guernsey militia; one from Henry Nail, who was with some of the wounded men the night following; and the other from a gentleman living in Mansfield at the time. Each differs in some essential particulars. Much experience has taught us that it is almost impossible to get perfectly accurate verbal narrations of events that have taken place years since, and which live only in memory."

Mr. Levi Jones was shot by some Greentown Indians in what is now the northern part of Mansfield, a few rods east of the Atlantic House, in August,

1813. He kept a store in Mansfield, and when the Greentown Indians left, refused to give up some rifles they had left as security for debt. He was waylaid, shot and scalped. The report of the rifles being heard in town, a party went out and found his body much mutilated, and buried him in the old grave yard. This was the last white man killed by Indians in the county of Richland, of which we have any account.

After the war, some of the Greentown Indians returned to the county to hunt, but their town having been destroyed, they had no fixed residence. Two of them, young men named Seneca John and Quilipetox, came to Williams' tavern, located at the southwest corner of the public square, opposite the site of the present Farmers' National Bank, in Mansfield, about noon; had a frolic, and quarrelled with some whites. About 4 o'clock in the afternoon they left, partially intoxicated. Those with whom they had qarrelled, five in number, went in pursuit, vowing revenge. They overtook them about a mile east of town, shot them down, and buried them at the foot of a large maple on the edge of the swamp, by thrusting their bodies down deep in the mud. The place of their interment is known to this day as "Spook Hollow."

"JOHNNY APPLESEED."

At an early day, there was a very eccentric character frequetly seen in Richland and the adjoining counties, well remembered by the early settlers. His real name was Jonathan Chapman, but he was usually known as *Johnny Appleseed*. He was originally, it is supposed, from New England.

Having imbibed a remarkable passion for the rearing and cultivation of apple trees from the seed, Johnny first made his appearance in western Pennsylvania, and from thence into Ohio, keeping on the outskirts of the settlements, and following his favorite pursuit. He was accustomed to clear spots in the loamy lands on the banks of the streams, plant his seeds, enclose the ground, and then leave the place until the trees had in a measure grown. When the settlers began to flock in and open their "clearings," Johnny was ready for them with his young trees, which he either gave away or sold for some trifle, as an old coat, or any other article he could use. Thus he proceeded for many years, until the whole country was in a measure settled and supplied with apple trees, deriving self-satisfaction amounting almost to delight, in the indulgence of his engrossing passion. After this county was well settled, he removed to the far west, there to enact over again the same career of humble usefulness.

His personal appearance was as singular as his character. He was a small "chuncked" man, quick and restless in his motions and conversation. His beard and hair were long and dark, and his eyes black and sparkling. He lived the roughest life, and often slept in the woods. His clothing was mostly old, being generally given to him in exchange for apple trees. He usually went bare-footed, and often travelled miles through the snow in that way. In doctrine, he was a follower of Swedenbourg—leading a moral, blameless life, likening himself to the primitive Chr stians,—literally taking no thought for the morrow. Wherever he went, he circulated Swedenborgian works, and if short of them, would tear a book in two, and give a part of it to different persons. He was careful not to injure any animal, and thought hunting morally wrong. He was welcome every where among the settlers, and treated with great kindness even by the Indians. We give a few anecdotes, illustrative of his character and eccentricities.

On one cool autumnal night, while lying by his camp-fire in the woods, he observed that the musquitoes flew in the blaze and were burnt. Johnny, who wore on his head a tin utensil which answered both as a cap and a mush pot, filled it with water and quenched the fire, and afterwards remarked, "God forbid that I should build a fire for my comfort, that should be the means of destroying any of his creatures." On another occasion he built his camp-fire at the end of a hollow log in which he intended to pass the night, but finding it occupied by a bear and her cubs, he removed his fire to the other end, and slept on the snow in the open air, rather than to disturb the bear. He bought a coffee bag, made a hole in the bottom, through which he thrust his head and wore it as a cloak, saying "it is as good as any thing." An itinerant preacher was holding forth on the public square in Mansfield, and exclaimed, "Where is the bare-footed Christian, travelling to heaven?" Johnny, who was lying on his back on some timber, taking the question in its literal sense, raised his bare feet in the air, and exclaimed *"here he is!"*

A LEGAL ANECDOTE.

The following singular legal anecdote is related as having occurred at New Philadelphia at an early day:

The court was held on this occasion at a log tavern, and an adjoining log stable was used as a jail, the stalls answering as cells for the prisoners.— Judge T. was on the bench, and in the exercise of his judicial functions severely reprimanded two young lawyers who had got into a personal dispute. A huge, herculean backwoodsman, attired in a red flannel shirt, stood among the spectators in the apartment which served the double purpose of court and bar-room. He was much pleased with the judge's lecture—having himself been practising at *another bar*—and hallooed out to his worship—who happened to be cross-eyed—in the midst of his harangue, "give it to 'em, old gimblet eyes!" "Who is that?" demanded the judge. He of the flannel shirt, proud of being thus noticed, stepped out from among the rest, and stretching himself up to his full height, vociferated "*it's this 'ere old hoss!*" The judge, who was always ready with a pungent repartee when occasion required, called out in a peculiarly dry and nasal tone, "Sheriff! take that *old hoss*—put him in *the stable*, and see that he is *not stolen* before morning."

RICHLAND COUNTY WHEN ORGANIZED, IN 1813.

At the organization of the county of Richland, in the spring of 1813, Samuel Watson, Melzar Tannehill and Samuel McCluer, were elected as County Commissioners, who held their first session in Mansfield, on June 7, of that year. From their recorded proceedings, we are enabled to gather some interesting facts connected with the early history of the county, not embraced in any of the historical sketches heretofore published.

The record shows that from six to nine of the 25 townships, as originally surveyed and numbered, were thrown together, forming but three municipalities or election districts, known as Madison, Jefferson and Green townships. On August 9, 1814, the county was divided into 4 townships, giving to the new one the name of "Vermillion," which embraced 12 by 18 square miles of territory in the northeast corner of the county, most of which is now in Ashland county. This left Green with 12 by 12 square miles in the southeast—Jefferson, 12 by 18, in the southwest, and Madison 18 by 18, in the northwest part of the county. So rapid was the increase of population in the county, that these four townships were soon subdivided and new ones formed out of the territory they had embraced. On the 5th of September, 1814, Troy was organized out of the north half of Jefferson, and Mifflin out of the west half of Vermillion, reducing each to 6 by 18 square miles. On June 6, 1815, Worthington was organized out of the west half of Green, and Montgomery out of the north part (two-thirds) of Vermillion, which reduced her to an original township, embracing 6 by 6 square miles. On March 4, 1816, Madison was reduced to her present boundaries by the organization of Bloominggrove and Springfield townships. The first was made to embrace 12 by 18 square miles in the northwest part of the county, while Springfield included the township afterwards known as Sandusky, two-thirds of which is now in Crawford county. On June 3, 1816, Orange township was formed out of the north half of Montgomery, reducing her to 6 by 6 square miles. Thus, in three years, the number had increased from three to eleven organized townships, four of which contained but 36 sections each. It is sufficient to state, in this connection, that at different sessions of the Commissioners afterwards, others were added to the number, until all the 25 townships, as originally surveyed and numbered, were separately organized.

We will now refer to some other interesting facts gathered from the recorded proceedings of the first board of County Commissioners.

Their first entry, (June 7, 1813,) is the appointment of Andrew Coffinberry as their Clerk. They then proceeded to levy the "chattel tax" for the year 1813, which was fixed at "30 cents for each horse or mare, and 10 cents for each head of neat cattle of a taxable age," which embraced all over 3 years old. From the same day's proceeding it appears that John Wallace filed his official bond as Sheriff of Richland county.

The first road entry was on the petition of William Gass and others for a

CLINE & RICE,

Manufacturers and Dealers in

BOOTS AND SHOES.

Main street,----SHELBY, OHIO.

We will be pleased to have any who have not dealt with us, give us a call; always ready to show customers through our stock, and satisfy them that

Our Prices are as Low as the Lowest!

We aim to keep a *GOOD CLASS OF GOODS*, a great portion of which WE ARE ABLE TO WARRANT.

Care in selecting stock, and employing none but the *Best of Workmen*, have built us up a LARGE MANUFACTURING TRADE, and it is our purpose to remunerate our patrons, by giving them GOOD WORK.

Our store is next east of the Jewelry Store. CLINE & RICE.

Thornton Hotel,

OPPOSITE THE

BALTIMORE & OHIO DEPOT,

A. C. THORNON, Proprietor,---Mansfield, O.

L. MORSE. J. C. PECK. S. H. ANDERSON. D. LOWRIE.

JUNCTION MILL COMPANY!

SHELBY, OHIO,

Commission Dealers and General Forwarders of all kinds of Grain, Manfacturers of

FAMILY, RYE, BUCKWHEAT & GRAHAM FROUR, CORN MEAL, SHORTS, FINE AND COARSE MIDDLIGS & CHOP FEED.

The Highest Price Paid for Wheat and all kinds of Grain.

Persons desiring to purchase *FIRST CLASS FLOUR*, can be accommodated upon short notice. **D. LOWRIE, Agent.**

road from the house of said Gass, to intersect the Delaware road at or near the present village of Lexington, where the mill of Amariah Watson was then being erected, on the Clear fork of Mohican.

[The William Gass above named, was the father of Benjamin, James R., William and Isaac Gass, and the three first named still reside within half a mile of the spot where their father then lived and continued to reside, till his death, in March, 1846.—Judge Gass was one of the pioneers of the county, having erected and occupied his cabin in 1811, but was compelled to remove his family to the vicinity of Mt. Vernon, until the Indian troubles had subsided. He was one of the first Associate Judges of the county—served for several sessions as a member of the Ohio Senate, and was universally respected both for his public services and private worth.]

THE FIRST COURT HOUSE.

On July 10, 1813, the Commissioners ordered that the block-house, standing a little south of the center of the public square, which had been erected for the protection of the early settlers against Indian depredations, be fitted up for the use of the county—the upper story for a court house, and the lower part for a jail. The carpenter work, being let to the lowest bidder, was awarded to Luther Coe, on August 4, 1813, for the sum of *forty dollars.* When the job was completed, the bill was paid out of a fund donated to the county by James Hedges, for the erection of public buildings in Mansfield.

[The contract for building our present court house, which succeeded the block-house, was made in 1826. Its cost, as fixed by the contract, was $3000. The new one, the corner stone of which was laid with appropriate ceremonies on September 27, 1870, is under contract at a cost of $177,000.]

On September 7, 1813, John Pugh was appointed Treasurer of Richland county, to fill the vacancy occasioned by the death of Levi Jones, who had been killed by Indians.

THE FIRST COURT OF RECORD.

In June, 1813, the first court of record within the county was held. It was a special session of the Common Pleas, held by the three Associate Judges, Peter Kinney, Thos. Coulter and Wm. Gass, for probate business.

The first Court of Common Pleas for general business, sat January 14, 1814. President Judge, William Wilson; Associates, Peter Kinney, Thomas Coulter and James McCluer; Clerk, Andrew Coffinberry; Sheriff, John Wallace. Our successive President Judges of the Court of Common Pleas, up to the formation of the Constitution of 1851, were Wilson, of Licking; Tod, (father of the late Governor,) of Trumbull; Harper, of Muskingum; Lane and Higgins of Huron; Dean and Cox, of Wayne; and Parker, of Richland.

The First Grand Jury, (empannelled January 14, 1814,) embraced the following persons: Isaac Pearce, George Coffinberry, Chrisley Brubaker, Thomas Lofland, Samuel Hill, Amariah Watson, George Crawford, Hugh Cunningham, Melzar Tannehill, Ebenezer Rice, Wm. Slater, Wm. Riddle, Solomon Lee and Rollin Weldon.

SHELBY
Hardware Store!

D. L. LOWRIE,

Has in store, and offers for sale at the

LOWEST CASH RATES,

A COMPLETE ASSORTMENT OF

FOREIGN AND DOMESTIC HARDWARE,

Consisting, in part, of

IRON AND STEEL AXELS, SPRINGS OF ALL KINDS. BOLTS,
HORSE SHOES AND HORSE SHOE NAILS, VICES,
BELLOWS, IRON, STEEL,

THE BEST NAILS IN MARKET.

STOVES, SHEET-IRON AND TINWARE,

GLASS—Both French and American.

Builders' Hardware in all its Various Branches.

MECHANIC'S EDGE TOOLS

*OF EVERY DESCRIPTION, AND FOR EVERY BRANCH
OF TRADE.*

Saws, Boring Machines, Chisels, Sadlery Hardware,

CARRIAGE TRIMMINGS,

HUBS, SPOKES, FELLOES, AND BENT STUFF, AT MANUFACTUR-
ERS PRICES.

A Splendid assortment of Table Cutlery, Pocket Knives, Razors and Plated Ware.

☞ Thanking the public for the liberal patronage heretofore received, I
intend by a strict application to business and fair dealing, to merit a con-
tinuance of the same. The Store is on the south side of Main, a few doors
west of Mickey's corner, Shelby, O.   D. L. LOWRIE.

The first resident lawyer of the county was John M. May, who, opening an office in Mansfield in 1815, died in the place within the last two years, at the age of eighty-two. James Purdy is the oldest surviving attorney in the county. He has been a member of the same bar for almost fifty years.

Having noticed the opening of the first court in Richland county, it will not be uninteresting, in this connection, to refer to the organization of

THE FIRST CIVIL COURT IN OHIO.

The first civil court ever convened in the territory northwest of the Ohio river, was held with imposing ceremonies, at Marietta, September 2d, 1788. We copy from the American Pioneer the following account of the organization and opening of the court:

" The procession was formed at the Point, (where most of the settlers resided,) in the following order:—1st, the high Sheriff, with his drawn sword; 2d, the citizens; 3d, the officers of the garrison at Fort Harmer; 4th, the members of the bar; 5th, the supreme judges; 6th, the governor and clergy; 7th, the newly appointed judges of the court of Common Pleas, Generals Rufus Putnam and Benjamin Tupper.

" They marched up a path which had been cut and cleared through the forest to Campus Maritus Hall, (stockade,) where the whole counter-marched, and the Judges, (Putnam and Tupper,) took their seats. The clergyman, Reverend Dr. Cutler, then invoked the divine blessing. The Sheriff, Col. Ebenezer Sproat, (one of nature's nobles,) proclaimed with his solemn 'O yes,' that a court is opened for the administration of even-handed justice, to the poor and the rich, to the guilty and the innocent, without respect of persons; none to be punished without a trial by their peers, and then in pursuance of the laws and evidence in the case.' Although this scene was exhibited thus early in the settlement of the state, few ever equalled it in the dignity and exalted character of its principal participators. Many of them belong to the history of our country, in the darkest as well as most splendid periods of the revolutionary war. The spectacle was witnessed by a large body of Indians, from the most powerful tribes then occupying the almost entire west, who had assembled for the purpose of making a treaty. Whether any of them entered the hall of justice, or what their impressions were, we are not told."

THE SUCCESSIVE OFFICERS OF RICHLAND COUNTY.

In giving a list of the officers of Richland County from its organization, in 1813, to 1870, we are unable to gather from the records the exact time of service of some of the first incumbents. Up to the year 1821, the County Commissioners and their Clerk seem to have performed all the duties which afterwards devolved upon the County Auditor. Several of the first County Treasurers were appointed by the Commissioners, and the taxes were paid to Collectors before they reached the Treasurer.

COUNTY TREASURERS.

Levi Jones,	1813 to 1813	David McCullough,	1856 to 1858
John Pugh,	1813 to	Thomas Willett,	1858 to 1860
Samuel Williams,		Thomas J. Robinson,	1860 to 1862
William Timberlake,		Thomas Willett,	1862 to 1864
Mordecai Bartley,		John M. Jolley,	1864 to 1866
Sylvanus B. Day,	1823 to 1836	Thomas J. Robinson,	1866 to 1868
John Murray,	1836 to 1842	Hugh W. Patterson,	1868 to
Robert Cowan,	1842 to 1846		

COUNTY AUDITORS.

James Hedges,	1821 to 1822
Andrew Conn,	1846 to 1852
John Stewart,	1822 to 1829
John P. Drennan,	1852 to 1856
Samuel G. Wolf,	1829 to 1833

COUNTY AUDITORS, Continued.

Benjamin Gass, ...	1833 to 1837
John S. Marshall,	1837 to 1841
John Meredith, ...	1841 to 1845
John M. Rowland,	1845 to 1849
Willard S. Hickox, ...	1849 to 1853
Jesse Williams, ...	1853 to 1857
John J. Douglass,	1857 to 1861
Jonas Smith, .	1861 to 1865
Jamuel Snyder, ..	1865 to 1869
Mark McDermot,	1869 to

CLERKS OF COMMON PLEAS.

Andrew Coffinberry,	1813 to 1815
Winn Winship,	1815 to 1820
Ellzey Hedges,	1820 to 1834
Jared Irwin, ...	1834 to 1838
Elijah W. Lake,	1838 to 1846
Wm. W. Irwin, ...	1746 to 1852
Calvin A. Croninger,	1852 to 1854
Wm. S. Higgins, ..	1854 to 1857
George B. Harmon, ...	1857 to 1857
Isaac Crum,	1857 to 1860
Eckels McCoy, ...	1861 to 1861
William Ritter, ...	1861 to 1867
George B. Harmon, ...	1867 to

SHERIFFS OF THE COUNTY,
With the date of their Election.

John Wallace, ...	1813
James Moore, ...	1816
Henry H. Wilcoxon, ...	1820
Samuel G. Wolf, ...	1825
Matthew Kelly, ..	1829
George Armentrout,	1833
John McCollough, .	1837
David Bryte, .	1741
William Kerr.	1743
Wm. B. Hammett,	1747
Frederick Warf, ...	1751
David Wise,	1855
George Weaver, ...	1859
John W. Strong,	1863
Isaac Fair, ..	1865
Robert Moore, ...	1869

COUNTY COMMISSIONERS.

Samuel McCluer,	1813 to 1814
Melzar Tannehill,	1813 to 1818
Samuel Watson, ...	1813 to 1820
Michael Beam, ..	1814 to 1820
Isaac Osbun, ...	1818 to 1820
Robert Bentley, ..	1820 to 1820
Barthol. Williamson, .	1820 to 1820
Alexander Curran,	1820 to 1821
Samuel McCluer,	1821 to 1823
James Hedges.	1821 to 1822
Linus Hayes,	1821 to 1830

Thomas Coulter, ...	1822 to 1824
James Heney, ...	1823 to 1824
Solomon Gladden, ..	1824 to 1830
Spooner Ruggles,...	1824 to 1831
James Larimer,......	1830 to 1836
John Oldshue,.	1831 to 1837
Wm. Taylor,	1832 to 1835
Henry Keith,	1835 to 1841
Joshua Canon,	1836 to 1842
Daniel Campbell.	1837 to 1843
Wm. Taggert,	1841 to 1847
Wm. B. Hammett, ...	1842 to 1845
John McCool, ...	1843 to 1848
Thomas B. Andrews,...	1845 to 1848
Jesse W. Davidson, ...	1847 to 1850
Robert Leech,.........	1848 to 1854
James W. McKee, ...	1848 to 1849
Thomas B. Andrews,.	1849 to 1854
Jont. Montgomery, ..	1850 to 1856
James Langham,......	1852 to 1854
Willard S. Hickox, ...	1854 to 1861
John Ramsey,	1854 to 1860
Charles Anderson, ...	1856 to 1859
Benjamin Morris,......	1859 to 1862
Leonard Swigart,......	1860 to 1866
James Thompson,..	1861 to 1867
Henry Cline,	1862 to 1868
David Taylor,	1866 to
John T. Keith, ...	1867 to
Daniel M. Snyder,	1868 to

COUNTY RECORDERS.

Andrew Coffinberry,	1813 to 1815
Winn Winship.	1815 to 1820
Matthias Day.. ..	1820 to 1832
John Reed,.... ...	1832 to 1838
Wm. W. Irwin, ...	1838 to 1844
James D. Summers,	1844 to 1847
James E. Cox, .	1847 to 1853
Eckels McCoy,	1853 to 1859
James E. Cox,	1859 to 1865
Elijah Clark, .	1865 to

PROBATE JUDGES.

Joel Myers, .	1852 to 1858
John Meredith, .	1858 to 1864
M. W. Worden,	1864 to 1867
Joel Myers,	1867 to

COUNTY SURVEYORS.

The following list embraces the successive County Surveyors, from the organization of the county:

First,	William Riddle,
Second,	John Stewart,
Third,	Christian Wise,
Fourth,	Warren Scranton,
Fifth,	John Newman.

THE FIRST JUSTICES OF THE PEACE OF RICHLAND COUNTY.

The following list of the early Justices of the Peace in Richland County, is made up from an old record embracing the date of their official oaths, as kept by the Clerk of the Court of Common Pleas. A few others may have had the oath administered to them by other officers, who omitted to certify the same to the Clerk. We give the names in the same order as they appear on the record, from 1813 to 1823:

1813. George Coffinberry, James McCluer and Josiah L. Hill.
1814. Wm. Riddle, Andrew Coffinberry, John Weiriek, Sam'l Hill, Wm. Taylor and Michael Beam.
1815. Wm. Gardner, Abraham Hetrick, Duncan Spice and John Palmer.
1816. Amariah Watson, Henry Daley, Richard Condon, Melzar Tannehill, Robert Ralston, Thomas Pope and Isaac Osbun.
1817. Wm. Holson, Jacob Cline, John Cook, Benj'n Montgomery, John Stewart, Daniel Johnson, Robert McBeth, Joseph Workman Andrew Ritchey, William Spier, Jacob Osbun, B. Williamson and Clement R. Pollock.
1818. John Williamson, Abraham Trucks, William Co'e, Cyrus Langworthy, James Huntsman, Nicholas Flaharty and Michael Shewey.
1819. Ephraim Eckley, John Young, Rich'd Grubaugh, Stephen Butler, Daniel Ayres, Samuel King, David Markley, Robert Nelson, Solomon Gladden, Jacob Crouse, Stephen Smith, Giles H. Swan, John Garrison and Geo. Marshall.
1820. Wm. Hoy, Jacob Mason, James Haverfield, James Doughty, Jehu Singery, Lynns Hayes, Michael Culler and Nathan C. Potter.
1821. Mordecai Bartley, Ebenezer Smith, Spooner Ruggles, A. D. W. Bodley, True Patee, John Shauck, James Henry, John B. Taylor, Isaac Armstrong, Ellzey Hedges, Robert Ekey and Jacob Cuykendall.
1822. Jeptha Dunn, John Mitchell, Ezra Williams, Jonas Cline, J. Coulter, Ahira Hill, Josiah Gallup, Rouse Bly and Jacob Myers.
1823. Harry Ayres, James R. Gass, Joseph H. Reed and David Hunter.

PIONEER LIFE IN RICHLAND COUNTY.

Not having settled in Richland county till 1818, five years after its organization, we have requested several of the older settlers to furnish for this work, an account of their *pioneer life.* The following is communicated by a PIONEER, who still resides in the county:

Judge Meredith:—In compliance with your request, I will endeavor to give you a brief sketch of early times in Richland county, derived from my own experience and observation.

When my parents reached this, which then formed part of Knox county, I was but a small boy, and will only attempt a mere sketch of the difficulties and privations with which the early settlers were compelled to contend.

On our arrival upon the piece of land, entered by my father the preceding summer, which was about three miles from any house or road, we slept the first night in the wagon which brought "our little all" from an older settled county. The weather being pleasant, nothing disturbed our repose, except the howling of the wolves and the responses made to them by our half-grown dog. The next day, we built a little shanty of poles, erected by the side of a large oak log, which formed one side of the little camp-house, in which we slept the second night. This camp was occupied as our home for several weeks, till a cabin, about 14 feet square, was built and covered

with clapboards. We moved into the cabin the latter part of April, without waiting for the puncheon floor and paper windows, with which it was afterwards embellished. No time was to be lost in preparing the forest for a patch of corn and potatoes. My venerable father, with the assistance rendered him by my brother, then 11 years old, and myself, two years younger, (and boys *worked* in those days,) then commenced our first clearing.— By the middle of June we had about an acre of ground cleared, enclosed with a temporary brush fence, and planted with corn, pumpkins and potatoes. This afforded us roasting-ears and potatoes by the first of September, and pumpkins in October. Our "truck-patch," with some two or three acres cleared beside it, were sown in wheat the same fall, which may be taken as proof that we were not idle the first summer. Our bread for the first six months, was made from two bushels of wheat and a few bushels of corn bought and ground at a mill in Knox county. Many of the early settlers, for want of money to buy grain, and for the want of mills to grind it after it was procured, were compelled to use hominy for days, as a substitute for bread. I knew one family whose diet for several weeks consisted of dried venison and milk. Those who owned a milch cow, could always have plenty of milk during the summer season, because the pasture in the woods, was then equal to a clover-field. Fresh meat was also easily obtained. A kind Providence had supplied the forest with a great many deer and turkeys. They served as food for the *red men*, and were well adapted to the wants of the white settlers. The bees, too, had their honey-stores in hollow forest trees, so that after we had sufficient land cleared to raise our bread and furnish provender for our cows, we imagined ourselves living on the borders of a land "flowing with milk and honey."

The principal clothing of the early settlers consisted of a hunting-shirt, made partly of wool and partly of flax or tow, with buckskin pants, for men and boys. The ladies made their summer dresses of flax, and those worn in the winter of flax and wool—all carded, spun and wove by themselves. I need but add, that ladies were just as attractive in their homespun dresses then, as they have ever been since *Paris Fashions* and foolish extravagance have become the order of the day.

It would be superfluous for me to attempt to give a detailed account of early times in Richland county. I have only referred to a few facts which came under my own observation, and will conclude my remarks by calling attention to the experience of a Pioneer of another county of this state, as narrated in his communication, published in Howe's History of Ohio. I copy his remarks, with slight variations, so as to make them applicable to many of the first settlers of this county, affording a better idea of *Pioneer Life* everywhere, than I would be able to give.

The writer says, " People who have spent their lives in an old settled country, can form but a faint idea of the privations and hardships endured by the pioneers of our now flourishing and prosperous state. When I look on Ohio as it is, and think of what it was in 1802, when I first settled here, I am struck with astonishment, and can hardly credit my own senses. When I emigrated, I was a young man, without any property, trade or profession, entirely dependent on my own industry for a living. I purchased 60 acres of new land on credit, two and a half miles from any house or road, and built a camp of poles 7 by 4 feet, and 5 high, with three sides, and a fire in front. I furnished myself with a loaf of bread, a piece of pickled pork, some potatoes, borrowed a frying-pan, and commenced housekeeping. I was not hindered from my work by company; for the first week I did not see a living soul, but, to make amends for the want of it, I had every night a most glorious concert of wolves and owls. I soon (like Adam) saw the necessity of a help-mate, and persuaded a young lady to tie her destiny to mine. I built a log-house, 20 feet square—quite aristocratic in those days—and moved into it. I was fortunate enough to possess a jack-knife; with that I made a wooden knife and two wooden forks, which answered admirably for us to eat with. A bedstead was wanted; I took two round poles for the posts, inserted a pole in them for a side rail, and two others for end pieces; the other end of each was put into a log of the house. Some puncheons were then split, which formed a substantial bed-cord, upon which we laid our straw bed—the only bed we had—on which we slept as soundly and woke as happy as Albert and Victoria.

In process of time, a yard and a half of calico was wanted; I started on foot through the woods, a distance of ten miles, to the nearest store, to procure it; but alas! when I arrived there, in the absence of both money and credit, I found that the calico could not be obtained. The dilemma was a serious one, and how to escape, I could not devise; but I had no sooner informed my wife of my failure, than she suggested that I had a pair of thin pantaloons, which I could very well spare, that would make quite a decent frock. The pants were cut up, the frock made, and the child dressed.

The long winter evenings were rather tedious, and in order to make time pass more smoothly, by great exertion, I purchased a share in a library, 6 miles distant. From this I promised myself much entertainment; but another obstacle presented itself:—I had no candles; however, the woods afforded plenty of hickory bark, which answered as a substitute. Many a night have I passed in reading to my wife till 12 or 1 o'clock, while she was hatcheling, carding or spinning. Time rolled on;—the payments on my land became due, and money, at that time, in Ohio, was a *cash article*:— However, I did not despair. I bought a few steers; some I bartered for, and others I got on credit—my credit having somewhat improved since the calico expedition—slung a knapsack on my back, and started alone with my cattle for Romney, on the Potomac, where I sold them—then travelled on to Litchfield, Connecticut, 600 miles distant, paid for my land, and had just one dollar left to bear my expenses home. By working at low wages, I added a trifle to my one dollar, and commenced my journey homewards, which I reached in safety.

I might enumerate similar scenes without number, which have passed under my own observation, or have been related to me by those whose veracity I have no reason to doubt; but from what I have written, you will be able to perceive that the path of the pioneer is not strewed with roses, and that the comforts which many of our inhabitants now enjoy, have not been obtained without persevering exertions, industry and economy. What, let me ask, would the young people of the present day think of their future prospects, were they now to be placed in a similar situation to mine in 1803? How would the young miss, taken from the fashionable, modern parlor, covered with Brussels carpets, and ornamented with pianoes, mirrors, &c., manage her spinning wheel, in a log cabin, on a puncheon floor, with no furniture, except, perhaps, a bake-oven and a split broom?"

I need but state in conclusion, that the first settlers of this county formed a kind of *social democracy* which is only exhibited in pioneer life. If a man was only able to purchase 40 acres of land, and paid for it by making rails for his neighbor, who owned a whole section, they met as equals. The only distinctions known to exist were such as would separate the very bad from the more intelligent and virtuous settlers. We all felt as one family, and took pleasure in relieving the wants and promoting the happiness of each other. To this day, I meet a pioneer as a *brother*.   OLD SETTLER.

POPULATION AND VOTE OF RICHLAND COUNTY.

The following table exhibits the population of Richland county in 1860 and 1870; to which is added the vote of the different townships for Governor in 1869, and the vote for Secretary of State in 1870.

Townships.	Pop. in 1860.	Pop. in 1870.	Loss.	Gain.	Rep. vote, 1869.	Dem. vote, 186).	Rep. vote, 1870.	Dem. vote, 1870.
Bloominggrove, ..	1360	1199	161		100	165	89	131
Butler,	1050	768	282		95	71	86	60
Cass,	1404	1291	113		131	141	124	122
Franklin,	1128	943	185		48	154	34	127
Jackson,	1025	945	80		52	131	51	108
Jefferson,	2388	2253	135		236	235	246	236
Madison,	1686	1521	165		154	181	118	163
Mansfield, (City,).	4581	8030			688	773	645	681
Mifflin,	963	901	62		53	120	25	106
Monroe	1765	1576	189		157	225	120	208
Perry,	825	686	139		62	93	56	84
Plymouth,	1771	1626	145		180	147	137	117
Sandusky,	688	688			41	84	24	57
Sharon,	1222	964	258		292	254	287	245
Shelby,(village,)..	1003	1816						
Springfield,	1756	1579	177		175	155	161	139
Troy,	1548	1312	236		159	118	150	148
Washington,	1797	1312	485		141	183	125	170
Weller.	1201	1140	61		119	92	112	68
Worthington,	1907	1878	119		101	275	89	232
Total,	31158	32428	2992	4262	2964	3595	2679	3207

(Mansfield gains 3449, and Shelby, 813.)

THE SUCCESSIVE NEWSPAPERS OF MANSFIELD.

The following list of Newspapers published in Mansfield since the organization of Richland county, is derived partly from our own recollection, and partly from the memory of other old settlers. We are unable either to give the year in which some of them made their first appearance, or the length of time they continued to be published.

The *Western Harbinger* was published by J. C. Gilkison and John Fleming. It is thought the first number was issued about the year 1817.

The *Mansfield Gazette* succeeded the Harbinger, and was published by Jas. and J H. Purdy, from 1823 to 1832. In this office we set our first type.

The *Sentinel* was published by Josiah F. Reed from 1829 to 1832, when it and the Gazette were merged into the Ohio Spectator.

The *Ohio Spectator* was published for a time by T. W. Bartley and Henry Layman; then by J. H. Hofman and J. Rentzel, till 1836, when we purchased the materials and commenced the publication of the Shield and Banner. In 1841, J. Y. Glesner purchased the establishment, and still continues to publish the paper without changing its title.

The *Richland Whig* was published by C. & J. Borland, from about 1833 to 1837. For near two years after the Whig was discontinued, the Shield and Banner, then conducted by us, was the only newspaper in Mansfield.

The *Richland Jeffersonian* was published by J. C. Gilkison & Son, about the year 1840. It was continued for a few years, when the Mansfield Herald became its successor. The *Herald* was conducted by M. Day and others, till purchased by L. D. Myers & Brother, by whom it is still published.

The *Richland Democrat* was published for some two or three years, commencing in 1848, by Joel Myers and Jacob Reisinger. A paper bearing the same title, was also published from 1857 to 1859, by L. C. Kelly & Co.

Besides the above, two campaign papers were published in Mansfield :--- one, entitled "The Penant," by W. L. Tidball, J. L. Tidball and J. Wiley; the other, by Wm. Johnson, entitled "The Bugle." They were both ably conducted sheets, but we cannot give the date of either.

At present we have nine newspapers within the territory formerly embraced in Richland county. Of these, 2 are at Mansfield, 2 at Ashland, 2 at Shelby, 1 at Plymouth, 1 at Crestline and one at Galion.

THE LATE CENSUS.—POPULATION OF OHIO BY COUNTIES.

Counties.	1870.	1860.	Counties.	1870.	1860.
Adams	21140	20309	Lorain	30438	29740
Allen	23546	19185	Lucas	44193	25831
Ashland	31922	22951	Madison	15636	13015
Ashtabula	32427	21814	Mahoning	30684	25894
Athens	23800	21364	Marion	16219	15490
Auglaize	29943	17187	Medina	20082	22517
Belmont	39913	34398	Meigs	31284	26534
Brown	30853	29958	Mercer	17268	14104
Butler	39653	35840	Miami	32747	29959
Carroll	14501	15788	Monroe	25813	25740
Champaign	24210	22628	Montgomery	60409	52230
Clark	32117	25300	Morgan	20247	22119
Clermont	34308	33034	Morrow	48581	50445
Clinton	21921	21461	Muskingum	45200	44416
Columbiana	38855	32830	Noble	19956	20751
Coshocton	23747	25032	Ottowa	13244	7016
Crawford	24588	23881	Paulding	8552	4945
Cuyahoga	133105	78033	Perry	18465	19678
Dark	30972	26209	Pickaway	24274	23469
Defiance	15722	11868	Pike	15540	13643
Delaware	25187	23902	Portage	24194	24208
Erie	28206	24474	Preble	21833	21820
Fairfield	31184	30531	Putnam	17104	12908
Fayette	17181	15935	Richland	32428	31158
Franklin	63524	50361	Ross	37090	35071
Fulton	17796	14043	Sandusky	25566	21428
Galia	25421	22040	Sciota	28385	24297
Geauga	13084	15817	Seneca	30846	30808
Green	29516	26197	Shelby	20754	17793
Guernsey	23903	24747	Stark	52608	42978
Hamilton	296617	116410	Summit	34986	27347
Hancock	23803	22886	Trumbull	38354	30656
Hardin	18615	13570	Tuscarawas	33866	32463
Harrison	18640	19110	Union	18660	16507
Henry	13928	8901	VanWert	15709	10238
Highland	29163	27773	Vinton	15047	13631
Hocking	17934	17057	Warren	26709	26902
Holmes	18176	20589	Washington	39979	36268
Huron	28525	29610	Wayne	35634	38483
Jackson	21859	17941	Williams	21028	16533
Jefferson	29191	26115	Wood	24671	17886
Knox	25405	27735	Wyandot	18563	15596
Lake	15953	15570			
Lawrence	30000	23249	Total	2,743,692	2,339,511
Licking	37707	37021			
Logan	23085	29990			

Several counties have lost since 1860, but the state gain is 404,181.

Many pages may yet be added to this work !

It will be seen by referring to the cover, that 500 pages, in Magazine form, *may* and in all probability *will* be added to this work.

Important Achievement!---A Grand Success!

When we commenced the publication of the *New System of Maps*, we were fully satisfied that the improvements made and secured to us by COPYRIGHT, were so *practical* and *important* as to enable us to furnish our patrons with a COMBINED MAP AND DIRECTORY, for $5, embracing more than double the information contained in any of the County Maps recently published by other authors, and sold at $10 per copy. Our anticipations have been more than realized. We not only give *double information for half price*, but it is presented in such a shape as to be obtained in less than one-tenth of the time heretofore required to find it. Besides producing what is conceded to be

THE BEST MAP FOR COUNTY PURPOSES EVER PUBLISHED,

It and the Directory, forming *one work in two parts*, supplies the place of and is more than equal in value to three large and expensive maps.

By the NEW FEATURES displayed on the face of the map, with the alphabetical arrangement of the names of persons and places on its margins and in the Directory, the miles and course to the residence of farmers in all parts of the county, to each county seat of the State, and to all the principal cities of the United States, are immediately ascertained, without making the map so large as to be inconvenient for reference.

With three large, old style maps before him, one for the County, another for the State, and a third for the United States, no man would be able to climb up and gather from all of them, more than half the practical information in an hour, which could be obtained in five minutes, without rising from his seat, by referring to our *combined County Map and Directory*.

This is not all. We have added to what is acknowledged to be THE MOST VALUABLE COUNTY DIRECTORY EVER PUBLISHED, a concise and interesting

HISTORY OF RICHLAND COUNTY FROM ITS ORGANIZATION.

It embraces a list of the County Officers from 1813 to 1870; the conflicts with Indians and other incidents connected with the *Pioneer Life of the Early Settlers;* the captivity of Col. James Smith: valuable Statistics, and other interesting matter, which every intelligent man, woman, boy and girl in the county, will be anxious to read and *preserve for future reference.*

Another important object has been accomplished. By inserting Business Notices on alternate pages, every person in the county is enabled to learn not only the *location of business men,* but where to BUY and where to SELL everything desired. The fact is just becoming known that our book affords

THE BEST ADVERTISING MEDIUM EVER INTRODUCED!

Never before did the BUSINESS MEN of this county, enjoy the privilege of securing room for their notices in a book which will be *wanted, read, preserved and referred to for years,* by nearly every family in the county. This feature of our work renders it necessary for us to publish

An addition to the Book, in Magazine form,

Which, when sent by mail to each subscriber, and bound with the pages already published, will form part of the same volume.

THE ADDITIONAL PAGES OF THIS WORK.

The necessity of enlarging this volume has already been stated. Until this *first part* is sold, we will neither know the number of copies wanted, nor the additional pages required, in Magazine form, to accomodate our patrons. Our friends who have examined the part already published, assure us that

The Combined Map, Directory and History,

Will be wanted by every intelligent person and family in the county. A copy of the book, at least, is expected to be ordered for every dwelling.

The quantity of valuable matter collected and now on hand, aside from what is still being furnished by *old settlers*, is sufficient of itself to make a large book. We will not promise to publish the whole of it;—but while BUSINESS NOTICES continue to be ordered and *paid for*, they will occupy alternate pages with such important matter as will be read with interest and carefully preserved, even if our volume should be swelled to

FIVE HUNDRED ADDITIONAL PAGES.

On the completion of the work, the *Index to the Advertisements* is expected to form a GRAND BUSINESS DIRECTORY, affording a ready reference to the LOCATION and BUSINESS of each individual who shall have ordered a notice. If any *Business Man, Manufacturer, Dealer* or *Mechanic* is not known to every family in the county, it will not be our fault, but his neglect to

Advertise before it is too late to secure room !

Having completed the most expensive part of the work, it will be sold at a price which will *cover cost*. The balance will be equally interesting, and can be obtained at a very trifling expense. Each number of the Magazine, containing 16 pages, will be mailed to subscribers at *only five cents*, payable to Post Masters, (who are authorized to act as our agents,) upon delivery.

We want a complete list of all the Pioneers !

Our list of the Pioneers of the different townships is not yet full. Will each *old settler* now living, furnish us the names of such persons as he may recollect as residents of the county prior to 1820 ? We also want the date of their settlement, and all interesting facts connected with early times.

To Canvassing Agents !

Our canvassing agents are expected to call at every house and truthfully explain the nature and importance of the *combined Map and Book*. The *price* places it within the reach of all, and every family capable of appreciating its value as a *work of reference*, will want a copy. Although a few individuals may only purchase *a part* instead of the *entire work*, we are assured that our LIST OF SUBSCRIBERS, when completed and published, will not only embrace the names of all who *now are*, but all who can ever reasonably expect to become *intelligent and useful citizens*. Give all a chance to enroll their names.

J. B. MEREDITH, Publisher.